A New Beginning

A New Beginning

LAURA RANDELL

IW
BOOKS

A New Beginning

Copyright © 2025 Laura Randell

All rights reserved.

ISBN: 978-1-0681889-3-0 (paperback)
        978-1-0681889-4-7 (ebook)

Published by: IW Books

Printed in the United Kingdom

Praise for *A New Beginning* from NetGalley Readers

"A charming, feel-good read... It's low on spice but high on heart—a perfect pick for fans of cinnamon bun heroes, forced proximity, and opposites-attract stories."

—Leanne H.

"I thought I'd read a chapter or two before bed—and suddenly it was 2 a.m., and I was emotionally tangled in Tamsin's world, rooting for her like she was a close friend who just needed one good break. The writing is warm and witty... It's the kind of book that wraps around you like a favorite sweater."

—Nathalie N.

"I love how strong and determined Tamsin was... these two are 'snuggle me in warmth' kind of romance reading. I just couldn't stop grinning."

—Kate T.

"It was so well written in the holiday romance element... The characters were so well done and I was invested in what was happening to them."

—Kathryn M.

"It had me hooked from page one... I loved this romcom!!!"

—Laura G.

ACKNOWLEDGEMENTS

Thank you JCS, for everything.
And thanks to Betsy, my first reader.

CHAPTER 1

Wednesday 6th November

"Red Brick Realty, selling London's luxury homes! Tamsin Davies speaking, how may I help you?!"

Oh God, please, please, please, be a serious person.

She noticed a snag in her panty-hose and, reaching down to look at it, knocked over her tea, spilling it on her desk and property sheets.

Lately, it seemed that every caller was intent on wasting her time. People were only calling to ask for a second opinion on the value of their home, not to make offers on houses or flats she had for sale.

After a long chat with a decidedly unserious person, she hung up the phone just in time to grab lunch before a two o'clock appointment in Oxford.

It would be her third journey from London to Oxford this week. She was going to show the chocolate box house called Lavender Cottage to a financially stable, loved-up couple from the city looking for a weekend bolt hole in a chic country location. Then she would show the lovely house to an overseas buyer who had flown all the way from New York just to see the cottage.

She'd have to smile nicely while she showed them all

around and listen to them say how charming it was, which really meant they thought it was small. To address that particular concern, she would say it was quaint.

Size seemed to be the main reason preventing people from buying the cosy cottage. From her point of view, size was the least important barrier.

The price was outrageous. Although technically, it *was* market value. The listing price was one million seven hundred thousand pounds. For only eight hundred square feet, Tamsin struggled to call it a good buy, but her manager, James, said it was an absolute steal at that price.

Even though most of the people she had shown it to were not interested in purchasing the cottage, and were just curious about what a two bedroom cottage in the world famous A-list favourite area of the Cotswolds looked like, there was always a chance they might be serious.

As long as she didn't have to hold any more sniffling barking dogs when showing the house, she could just about manage the long drive to Oxford.

Walking down the street, distracted, and wondering why she went into the estate agency business in the first place, Tamsin tripped on the pavement, crashed into a fellow passerby and dropped her mobile.

She picked up her phone, turned it over and saw that the glass screen had shattered into lines that looked like a spider's web. Picking it up gingerly, and hoping it would still work, she placed it into her bag.

Just what I need!

Standing in line for a salad at Chez Paris, she suddenly heard a voice that seemed familiar, coming from behind her.

"Tamsin, TAMSIN, darling, is that you? Over *here*, dear."

Tamsin turned around, and, standing a few people behind her in line, just far enough so that she'd have to get out of the queue to talk to her, was Philippa Smythe-Jones, toy dog lover extraordinaire.

Mrs. Philippa Smythe-Jones of Tansley Hall, or Lady Philippa as she was rightly referred to, had been to see the property in Oxford two weeks before. As soon as they had entered the house, Lady Philippa had placed her barking terrier in Tamsin's hands, while she carried on walking through the house alone, ignoring Tamsin, who followed along behind her. Lady Philippa hadn't said a word, and just kept shaking her head with disapproval at everything she saw.

When Tamsin felt she could finally put the dog down, he ran in and out of the house and then around in circles. Tamsin had to clean up the dog's muddy paw prints left all over the floor. She was trying to put the experience out of her mind.

"Hello, Lady Philippa," said Tamsin.

"Oh dear, it's so terribly *dreary* out today, isn't it?"

Even for early November the weather was awful in London. It was colder than usual and drizzling rain.

"Yes," Tamsin mused, not really listening. She realized it was now too late to get lunch at all. With rain falling and fog rolling in, she'd have to leave very soon to make it on time to show the Oxford property.

"My dear, has that darling little cottage sold?"

"Not yet. I'm on my way to show it right now."

"I'd love to see it again. Would I be able to join you?"

"I'm afraid not," Tamsin said, rather too quickly. Then, realizing she had sounded rude, she added, "I'm taking a client with me from London." It was a lie, since she was meeting both prospective buyers at the cottage.

But the idea of driving Lady Philippa all the way to Oxford, along with her dog, was more than Tamsin could handle at the moment.

Feeling guilty, she said, "I'd be happy to show it to you another time. Are you planning to make an offer on the cottage?"

Tamsin desperately hoped the answer would be yes. Her rent was due in a few days, and she could barely afford to pay it, never mind cover all her other living expenses.

Selling real estate was a very difficult job, as she'd found out. Most clients were friendly, and treated her like the professional she was, but some treated her like a servant, which she most certainly was not. The amount of time it took to sell something and see payment for it was making it impossible for her to manage her finances properly.

She had thought, as obviously so many other people also did, judging by the number of estate agents in London, that selling real estate was a great career option and even a quick way to make a lot of money. She'd had fantasies of how she'd spend her money, which she should have lots of by now – by her calculation – yet she didn't. After all, it looked so easy.

Things had started out well a year ago. She'd managed to join a top estate agency, which was an achievement, because competition was very fierce at high street firms.

And Tamsin wasn't working for just any firm. She was working at Red Brick Realty, in the very high end Sloane

Square, where a coffee cost six pounds. She had expected to do well right from the start, but she was naïve.

Reality soon kicked in that most of London's top earning estate agents were also from highly connected families, or had been doing it for so many years that they had grown their client lists organically, through referrals and repeat customers. She would never get to the stratospheric level of earnings she knew some people made. She was sure of that.

But even just a normal – reliable – salary would do. That was what she needed. Being an estate agent was also a lonely business. Most of the time she was on her own, in her car, or taking the tube because her car was in for repairs.

She couldn't afford the cost of cabs, mini-cabs or Ubers, and when her car was in for service and she had buyers to take around, it was a problem, because they expected someone working in Kensington to have a Merc.

"What was that, Lady Philippa?" Tamsin nearly had to shout to be heard, now that the lunch crowd had swelled in number and the long queue was out the door onto the pavement. Since everyone was now back to work at least a few days a week after Covid, familiar, decently priced places like Chez Paris were humming.

"I said, I'd like to bring my grandson Harry to see the cottage. He is a chef and needs a place to live in Oxford, because commuting from Kensington is untenable," said Lady Philippa.

"Yes, of course," said Tamsin, only half listening and thinking how nice it must be to live in Kensington.

The line was barely moving and Tamsin realized she had no more time to wait for food.

"I really must go, but can you meet me on Saturday at two, at Lavender Cottage? That is, if it hasn't sold by then," Tamsin said.

"Wonderful, dear. We'll meet you there," said Lady Philippa.

Tamsin waved goodbye as she left the café and walked quickly down Kings Road, trying to avoid the rain. Having forgotten a scarf, she pulled her coat collar up to keep the wind from her neck.

She hurried back to the office to get her laptop and car, hoping she had a muesli bar in her desk to stave off hunger until dinner.

CHAPTER 2

"Marvellous," said Tamsin to her client, barely able to contain her excitement.

David Herrington had just seen the cottage, and, after having a quick lunch, he had returned and now wanted to make an offer. He'd seen it twice this week, and was heading back to America, so wanted to have an agreement before his flight later in the day.

"I will call your offer in immediately," Tamsin said.

Tamsin added up the commission she would make on the sale of the cottage, and considered the ways she'd be able to spend the proceeds. But she quickly realized that after paying all her due and past due bills, she'd have little left. She was sinking deeper every month into a financial hole.

"Do make sure he understands this is a once and final offer," David said in his very distinctive New York City accent.

"Yes, of course," Tamsin said, while worrying that the offer he was making wasn't high enough and that the seller would never agree to it. She went to her car to make the call and get her laptop.

"My client is very interested in Lavender Cottage, Mr. Crighton," she said to the owner. "He absolutely adores the pond, the garden and the entire property. He's offering a very reasonable price and it would certainly be prudent to consider it," Tamsin said, hoping he couldn't hear how desperate she was for him to accept it.

Knowing there was an issue, and wanting to get it out of the way as quickly as possible, she said, "The only caveat is that he cannot complete the transaction for six months. I realize that is well beyond your timeline, and that you are all settled in Spain now. But the market conditions have changed significantly since the house first came on the market. Since we have not had an offer for three months, I encourage you to consider this one seriously," Tamsin said with as much authority as she could.

"What did he say?" David asked when she walked back into the cottage from her car.

"He said he will think about it and get back to us, which is encouraging," she said, trying to keep him interested and knowing that it was unlikely Mr. Crighton would accept the offer.

Needing to break the bad news, she continued, "Although, he isn't particularly happy about the six month period you have requested before being able to take the property. Is it at all possible for you reduce that by a month or two?" Tamsin asked.

"No. There are lots of other nice cottages to choose from and I won't be pushed into accepting terms I don't like," David said.

"Of course not. I understand," Tamsin said, sorry to have asked.

David Herrington was a wealthy, assertive business

man who was looking for a place for his daughter to live when she started at Oxford University in the spring, and he wanted to be in control of the situation.

"I'll call you as soon as I hear back from the seller," Tamsin said as cheerily as she could. Even though a lot of people were wasting her time asking to see a cottage they had no intention of buying, there had been four offers, including one at the asking price, which the seller had turned down.

This latest offer was for much less, so Tamsin thought the chances of it being accepted were low. She calculated in her head how much petrol and wear on her car this property was costing. It was much more than she should be spending.

But having invested so much time travelling back and forth to Oxford, she wanted to make the sale. In fact, she desperately needed to sell something, or she would be bankrupt by Christmas.

As of now, she didn't have enough money available to buy gifts for Christmas, never mind go back to university, which was her plan for the new year. Maxing out her credit card would be the only option, but then she'd be in a worse state financially.

Her mum and dad were really looking forward to seeing Tamsin for Christmas, and they expected her to come home for at least a week, if not two. She couldn't let them down. Although she went home to Margate regularly, she could always spend the most time with them at Christmas. The office was closed for ten days, and Tamsin would be bored in her flat on her own.

If she was going to make any money before the end

of the year, she would have to sell some real estate this month. It didn't seem likely.

But isn't Christmas all about miracles? she thought. Anything could happen in real estate, so she tried to think positively.

At Christmas, her parents always went over the top with everything. They loved decorating the house and the tree, and her mum made too much food. They also had a way of embarrassing Tamsin, by gushing to all their relatives how proud they were of her.

Tamsin dreaded the annual family gathering, since she hadn't lived up to her expectations of herself, never mind anyone else's. Of course, her parents didn't see it that way, and they were immensely proud of whatever she did.

But not having enough money to pay her increasing rent from the new year was making Tamsin quite worried and she had started to feel like a failure, even though she knew this was just a temporary blip.

She could talk to her parents about the financial troubles she was facing, but she didn't want to worry them. Her dad had a pension, and her mum had stayed home to raise Tamsin, so they couldn't afford to offer her any financial support.

Telling them she was in trouble would not be right. They were the best parents ever, and Tamsin loved them both deeply. She'd keep things to herself for now, until she had a plan.

When Tamsin's mum had last visited her, she'd said that Tamsin looked unwell, observing how tired she was, and resolved that the solution was for Tamsin to go back to uni, and finish her studies in law.

But Tamsin had written that off as an option and wasn't listening to her mum's advice, mostly because she had no way to pay for university and was embarrassed to say so. Since then, she had applied to and been accepted for law at City University, but the financial pressure her ex-boyfriend Jason had just put her under was making that dream impossible to consider or achieve. He was doubling the rent in six weeks, and she could not afford to pay it.

Tamsin wished that her mum would offer her old room back to her, so she could move home and not have to pay rent. Then she could go back to uni. She could just ask her mum and dad if she could move back in. She knew they would say yes, because they would love to have her living at home with them. But every time this idea came into her head, Tamsin got depressed thinking about having to move home at thirty-four to live with her parents.

The way things were going, she would never be able to pay off her sizable student loan from her art degree or get a chance to go back to university and become a barrister. It was all too much to think about, so she pushed the thoughts aside.

After locking up the cottage, Tamsin drove to the Poacher's Den pub to get something to eat before heading back to London. She was hopeful, but not convinced, that her seller would accept the fifth offer she had just presented to him on Lavender Cottage. She wanted to have something to eat, and enjoy a nice glass of wine before getting back on the road to London.

CHAPTER 3

As she walked into the pub, soaking wet from the rain which had begun to fall as soon as she had left the cottage, she looked around for somewhere to sit, but there were no tables available.

Tired, hungry and feeling overwhelmed by the crowded pub, she managed to squeeze herself in between some people at the bar and dropped her coat and bag on the floor.

The call with Mr. Crighton could have gone better, she thought.

He'd basically said no to the offer, as he had said to the other four she had presented to him.

Why he was being so difficult, when it was not as if he needed the asking price, Tamsin did not understand.

The owner of Lavender Cottage, Cyril Crighton, had come to the United Kingdom the year before as a visiting lecturer at Oxford, and had bought the house on a whim. He had never lived in it, because he was constantly travelling back to his native Australia, or to other cities around the world on his lecture tour.

When Tamsin saw the cottage for the first time, she had recommended that he make some minor improvements, such as clearing up the leaves, fixing the rising damp on the main floor, and making it look welcoming.

But he wasn't interested in fixing anything, so it was no wonder it was taking the cottage so long to sell. All people could see were problems. Yet, she had still managed to get five good offers and he was being completely unreasonable by not accepting any of them. It was as if he didn't really want to part with the cottage. But why that was, Tamsin had no idea.

The yard was overgrown with weeds which had shot up everywhere throughout the summer. All the leaves had since fallen from the trees, and no one was maintaining the yard. Tamsin had asked Mr. Crighton to hire someone to tidy the garden and fix the front gate, but since he had now retired and moved to Spain, he was even less interested than before in her ideas for how to sell the cottage. Today it had been such a shambles outside that she thought she might have to hire someone herself to clean things up.

Tamsin didn't know what it would take to convince Mr. Crighton to sell the lovely cottage. She would need to ask him what the issue was with selling it if he rejected the latest offer, and she may need to ask her boss, James Tomkin, to help.

Tired of thinking about it, and desperate for food and drink, she looked around for someone to take her drink order and provide her with a menu.

"Excuse me," said Tamsin, waving her hand up in the air as a means to get anyone's attention behind the bar.

"Yes, what can I get you?" the bartender asked, after helping several other people first.

"Can I please have a menu?" Tamsin asked. "And a dry white wine."

After a hearty meal of fish and chips, and feeling

relaxed for the first time in ages, she thought how cozy the pub was, and how beautiful Oxford was. Each time she came here she drove a different route through the town. It was the best way to find interesting things to point out to the buyers, like where the Michelin star restaurants were, the sailing club, the golf courses and all the schools.

People seemed very friendly in Oxford, and they obviously had fun. The pub was packed at four o'clock on a Wednesday afternoon in November, so they were obviously doing something right, and they were not making work the centre of everything in life. Totally unlike London, where it seemed all people did was work.

As she finished her drink, Tamsin dreaded getting on the motorway to make the long drive back to London.

"Do you mind?" someone asked Tamsin.

"What did you say?" Tamsin asked, turning to the sound of the voice. Looking up, she saw a tall blond man about her age, wearing jeans, a plaid shirt and muddy boots.

"I asked if you'd mind if I join you. There's nowhere else to sit," he said, tossing his head back towards the room, which was now completely full.

"Yes, ok," Tamsin said, reluctantly.

She removed her bag from the chair beside her, which she had taken hold of when it had become free, and she put it back on the floor. She was so tired, she felt as though she must have dozed off. It was clear the stranger had asked more than once about sitting down.

"Ben," he said, holding out his hand for her to shake.

"Tamsin," she said.

"If you don't mind me saying, you look awfully tired and downtrodden. Is everything ok?" he asked.

"Yes, I am. I mean, it is. Ok, I mean. I'm fine, thank you."
Ugh.

"In fact, I should be going," she said, sliding off the bar chair.

"Why not have a cup of coffee?" he suggested. "Get your eyes open." His blue eyes twinkled and shone at her.

She knew caffeine would help, so she agreed.

"Good idea. I've a long drive so it might do me some good."

He waved the bartender over and ordered a pint for himself and a black coffee for her.

"Where are you off to?" Ben asked.

"London."

"For work, or pleasure?"

"Both. I live and work there."

"What brings you up here to Oxford?" Ben asked.

"Also work." Not wanting to sound rude, but not wanting to keep answering questions, she asked him, "What about you? Do you live here in Oxford?"

"Part time. I've been travelling for a while."

Fascinated by the story he told her of trekking through the jungle in Thailand, and eating amazing cuisine all over Asia, Tamsin was reluctant to leave. But realizing it was getting dark, and knowing she'd now have to drive at night, which she hated, Tamsin said, "That must have been really incredible. I've always wanted to do something like that, travelling around the world."

"Why haven't you?"

"Life. Responsibilities. You know," she said, putting her coat on. "I have to go," she said, holding out her hand to shake his. He took it and she said, "It was nice meeting and talking to you." She hadn't meant to sound so formal, but he was a stranger, and she was tired.

Ben got up from his chair and looked directly at Tamsin, with his powder blue eyes that looked like the sea.

"Do you come to Oxford regularly?" he asked, clearly wanting her to stay longer.

"Yes. Unfortunately," she said as she rolled her eyes. "I'm working on something, so I do come here frequently. At least, for now. But that should end very soon."

"Would you like to join me for a drink the next time you're in Oxford? Or we could have dinner?" he asked.

Tamsin wasn't in the mood for meeting a new man. He'd only find out what a mess she was, the relationship would go nowhere, and that would be that.

"I don't think so, but thank you for asking. And good luck with everything. Goodbye!" she said cheerily and started walking towards the door.

"Bye," he said, raising his hand to wave at her, but she had already turned her back to him.

❋ ❋ ❋

As she drove back to London, Tamsin seemed to go in and out of a daydream.

Missing her exit, she was furious with herself for staying back to talk to Ben, instead of getting on the road earlier.

Ben had been charming. And good looking. And he was interesting, she thought to herself, while she tried to focus.

It was now very dark and raining hard. The wipers could barely keep the rain off the windscreen.

She had been driving for an hour and just wanted to get home.

Trying to stay calm, she thought about having a soak in the bath. She'd pair it with a glass of chilled white wine, which she had put into the fridge before she left London in the morning, and she longed to read the latest edition of *OK Magazine.*

Wine and glossy magazines were the perfect remedy for a bad day. But as she approached her exit off the A4, she could think only of having an early night and her head hitting the soft pillow that awaited her return.

CHAPTER 4

Saturday 9th November

Before starting her drive to Oxford to show Lavender Cottage to Lady Philippa, Tamsin went for a long run by the River Thames. She liked to run without music, so she could think. She thought about how much she loved living in Hammersmith, even though sometimes at night she did feel a bit unsafe. There were a few theatres and lots of bars, and on weekends it could get very busy.

It was easy getting around London from Hammersmith, which was a fantastic, convenient place to live. Tamsin would never be able to afford a place here on her own, however. And now she had to move.

Before she had met Jason, she had lived with friends in a house share in Tottenham. That had suited her just fine, but a few months after she and Jason had started dating, he asked her to move in to his flat, and she did. It was steps to the river and the flat was large and airy.

Jason was a qualified GP and worked as a junior doctor at Guy's and St. Thomas' Hospital when they met. But he had decided to become a barrister, and was just about to start the two years of full-time study he needed to qualify, when Tamsin moved in.

She was thrilled for him, but also for herself. All the night shifts and on-call work of a GP in a hospital meant they didn't see each other as much as they wanted to. He was always coming in as she was going out, or the other way around. With her working days at a gallery in Soho, and Jason being at university, it seemed like the perfect arrangement.

How wrong they had been about that.

The idea was that when Jason landed a job as a barrister, he would support them, and Tamsin could go back to university herself. She had to do one year of the bar vocation course full time and then a year of pupillage, before she too would be a qualified barrister, which was Tamsin's dream. For one reason or another, it had been thwarted over the years.

Tamsin had big ideas about helping people and winning cases in court, so succeeding at becoming a barrister was non-negotiable.

When Tamsin was choosing what to study at university as an undergrad, she had considered law, but had instead chosen an art degree, because she loved Renaissance art and wanted to enjoy university and have fun before doing the extra years to qualify as a barrister.

She regretted taking that approach now, because she knew that the two years she still needed to put in to become qualified were slipping further out of her reach as each day passed.

Tamsin now had a very sizable debt from her degree, and was only able to pay the minimum amount due each month. She had trusted that Jason would start supporting them both as soon as he qualified and found a job. She couldn't have been more wrong. But being naïve enough to trust him was what bothered her most.

After Jason graduated and started working full time at the Magic Circle law firm of Lyle and Evans as a barrister, just after Covid ended, Tamsin applied for the next intake at both City University and the University of Law, and was accepted to both.

She was getting ready to start her journey of becoming a barrister, had told her parents and all her friends, and was counting the days until uni started.

What she didn't know at the time, was that Jason's secretary, Amber, was the real reason he was always late coming home. It wasn't dinners with partners and clients as he had said.

When she found this out, entirely by accident, she was heartbroken. She had jumped out of the shower to pick up a ringing phone, which turned out to be Jason's. On the screen was a message with hearts and kisses. After the hurt came the anger that she was being made a fool of.

Their relationship ended abruptly and painfully after she saw that message. Jason tried to say the message was not for him, as if it had been sent to the wrong number, but he eventually admitted that he had been seeing someone else for months. Tamsin was devastated.

Since the flat was Jason's, or more accurately, his father's, she couldn't ask him to leave, but she had nowhere to go.

Jason said he would move out, and Tamsin agreed to pay rent. It was unjust, because she felt that all the money she had spent over the previous two years covering all of their expenses while he studied full time should count for something, but Jason didn't seem to care. He wanted market rent as well, which was a big stretch financially for Tamsin, and which she imagined he was spending on his new girlfriend.

To support them both, Tamsin had left a job she loved at a wonderful gallery in Soho, in order to take a higher paying job in a place she didn't like working, just so Jason could finish his degree.

It was hard for Tamsin to think about the situation and running helped her reduce the anger she felt at the injustice of it all.

Jason had obtained his legal qualification and landed an important job at a prestigious law firm, while Tamsin had achieved nothing in the last four years. She hated how he had lied to her, and tricked her into supporting him, and she felt used.

Since he had moved out, Jason had married his secretary, Amber, and she was about to have a baby. He'd called last week and told Tamsin that he would be doubling the rent from January, and if she could not pay it, he would need to sell the flat.

When she asked why this was necessary, or urgent, he said that the baby was due soon, Amber wanted a six bedroom house in Sevenoaks, and selling the flat in Hammersmith was the only way to get it. Tamsin was crushed.

Tamsin had already needed to increase her salary to cover the rent as it was, which is why she left the art world and had decided to get a job in property sales.

But in the last twelve months of working as an estate agent, she had not made any commissions, and was relying on her paltry salary to get by. It would not be enough each month to pay her student loan and the rent that was doubling, never mind food and transport.

She had six weeks left to earn enough to pay Jason what he was demanding every month. Otherwise, she would have to move back into her parents' house, or somewhere less expensive. The pressure was on to sell Lavender Cottage and anything else she could find that was languishing on the books of the estate agency.

Tamsin had gone through all the listings they had, and found that Red Brick Realty had two flats for sale in Shoreditch, which she thought were the best ones to try to sell.

She knew the area well, and she could talk up the neighbourhoods' good features, like where to eat, get a haircut or do yoga. She'd decided she would call the sellers of each flat on Monday and tell them she would personally be focussing on selling their properties.

As she came to the end of her run along the river, Tamsin thought how lucky she was to have a car. Most people did not. Her parents had bought it for her when she graduated from university, which she had appreciated very much, knowing it would have cost them dearly to pay for it. Now the car was more than ten years old, but still in great condition. The only problem was that it no would no longer pass an MOT and cars as old as hers were not supposed to be on the road in London. Compared to her other problems though, failing an MOT seemed like a minor issue, which she would continue to ignore.

It had been a while since Tamsin had time for a run by the river, and she always felt so good afterwards that she made a mental note to do it more often. When she got home, she showered, danced around the flat, singing, and once she had dried her hair sufficiently, she packed her laptop bag and hold all. Singing was a passion but she was doing less of that than usual recently.

For the journey to Oxford, she packed an extra jumper, a waterproof jacket, a scarf and gloves, and her wellies. She wasn't sure she needed the wellies, so she put them in and took them out of her bag twice. Then she remembered that the last time she was in Oxford she had been caught in a downpour and had ruined her shoes. This time she was wearing smart trousers instead of a skirt, and would change her heels for boots before she approached the cottage. She wasn't going to be caught in the rain or cold again without being prepared.

If she left soon, she would have enough time for a nice lunch before meeting Lady Philippa and her grandson Harry at the cottage. A relaxing pub lunch would put her in just the right mood to handle what she suspected would be another wasted journey.

CHAPTER 5

After a stressful drive on the motorway, the rest of the journey into the town of Oxford always made Tamsin relax, and today was no exception. The town was very pretty and vibrant.

It reminded her of Bristol, where she'd gone to university. She had fond memories of those days, and all her friends, of whom only Nico was in London.

Maybe it was the river, or just how *green* Oxford was, or the romantic buildings and the history of the place, but whatever it was, Tamsin had fallen in love with Oxford over the last several months. She didn't think she could ever settle here herself, but it was a beautiful place to live.

The journey from London to Oxford was normally busy, but on a Saturday morning in November it was quieter than usual. Most people with second homes in the area didn't go there frequently or at all during the late autumn, so the motorway wasn't the blur of taillights she was used to in weekday traffic or in summer. That took some of the stress away, at least for this journey.

One of her colleagues, Lottie, had given her the listing for Lavender Cottage six months earlier, not having been able to sell it herself and giving up after three months.

Tamsin thought it was a gift to be given a listing, but

now, she knew better. If she could give it to someone else, she would, but she had been so close to selling it multiple times, and was convinced that it would sell any day now.

The owner of the cottage, Mr. Cyril Crighton, had been a student at the same boarding school as her employer, James Tomkin, the owner of Red Brick Realty. So when Mr. Crighton decided to buy a cottage and then sell it within twelve months, he called his old friend James to help him, even though James and his team of estate agents were all based at their office in Chelsea.

James was one of the most respected property agents in London. He owned over eighty properties spanning the home counties, London and Edinburgh, and he could have bought the cottage himself and rented it out very quickly. That's what everyone else with expendable income seemed to be doing up and down the country, buying and renting out two and three bedroom cottages located in picturesque settings across Britain.

Or he could have finished refurbishing it and then sold it for even more than the current asking price. In any case, he would have had a great asset that could be making money, rather than an albatross, sitting miles away from London, that no one wanted to bother travelling to in order to sell it.

As she approached the University of Oxford, Tamsin drove past the gorgeous and imposing Ashmolean Museum and pulled into the now familiar Poacher's Den parking area. She'd made good time and had enough left before her appointment to sit down for a lovely lunch.

As she walked into the pub, Tamsin felt calm and immediately warm and cozy. There was a fire blazing in the grate, and a murmur of low voices. The daily specials on the board included dessert of crème brûlée, her favourite.

The pub was dark, with low beams, and filled with locals. The smell of wood burning from the open fire reminded her of her childhood, when she would sit next to her grandmother as she sat knitting in her rocking chair, while Tamsin had a hot cocoa and watched with wonder how the two metal sticks created jumpers in beautiful colours.

She started to well up with tears and quickly composed herself. Why Oxford was causing this emotional flood was a mystery to Tamsin. She had no roots in this neck of the woods. Her family on both sides were miners and fisher-men, not farmers.

Tamsin ordered the usual standby of fish and chips, and loved how they did the mushy peas in this pub. She thought it would be great if there was more healthy food nearby, but felt that eating the odd meal out with chips was alright.

Tamsin would normally have looked for a vegan restaurant, in an effort to cut down on meat, but the one vegan restaurant she had tried in Oxford she didn't like. Her favourite vegan places were in Bristol where she knew the menus by heart.

There were some amazing restaurants in Oxford, but they were all well outside her price range, including an Ethiopian one she desperately wanted to try. But even if she could afford it, she didn't have anyone to go there with, and it seemed to Tamsin that cuisine served in multiple dishes should be shared with others. She loved eating food served in small portions. Jason had never liked meals with small plates, so they never had tapas or cuisine to share with others. She missed the joy of tucking in with friends.

The last time she'd done so was with Becca, when they went for Indian food after work one day before the pandemic. They used to meet once a week after work until Covid changed everyone's life and now she rarely saw her. She could still recall the flavours and the scents of the food they had eaten the last time they had dinner together at Simran's.

Tamsin made a mental note to call Becca soon, since they hadn't seen each other for a while.

After dessert, Tamsin was full and didn't want to work, fancying a punt on the river instead. She had come to Oxford seven times in the last few months, and had never taken a ride on the river in the famous boats.

Maybe next time, she thought to herself.

If all went well, this would be her last trip to Oxford, at least for work.

CHAPTER 6

As she drove up the drive to Lavender Cottage, Tamsin wondered if she was seeing things. Standing outside the cottage was Lady Philippa, as expected, but next to her was the man Tamsin had met on Tuesday in the pub. Ben.

Hadn't Lady Philippa said she was bringing her grandson Harry to see the cottage?

"Fancy seeing you here," said Ben as Tamsin got out of her car.

"Hello," said Tamsin, smiling. "Good afternoon, Lady Philippa."

"Do you two know each other?" she asked them both, looking rather confused.

"Sort of," said Ben, before Tamsin could speak. "We met last week at the Poacher's Den."

"Nice to see you again, Ben," said Tamsin.

"Harry," said Lady Philippa. "This is my grandson Harry. His given name is Benjamin, but I have always called him by his second name, Harry, after my late husband."

"I see," said Tamsin as she opened the cottage door.

"After you, Ben. Harry. What should I call you?" Tamsin asked.

"Ben is fine," he said, as he stepped into the house.

Totally perplexed about what had just happened, but

mindful to show the house as well as she could, she said, "Welcome to Lavender Cottage! This is the loveliest cottage in our inventory and is far superior to any others on the local market either in Oxford or in the surrounding area."

"Hmm," said Ben.

After a walk through the cottage, Tamsin asked, "So, Lady Philippa, what you do think, now that you have seen the cottage again?"

"It is quite small, which is as I remembered, but it could suit Harry perfectly. What do you think, Harry?"

He didn't speak, so Tamsin suggested they make their way through the property again, followed by a walk in the grounds. She hoped that Ben and his grandmother would love it and make an offer before they left.

They walked through each of the bedrooms, slowly this time, and Tamsin pointed out the large original fireplaces and the herringbone flooring before they all moved into the garden to look at the pond.

Tamsin was worried that the state of the weeds, which were now over two feet tall, would put Ben off, but he didn't seem to mind. He didn't seem interested either, so she finally asked,

"Well, Ben, what do you think of this house? Can you see yourself living here?"

"It's a great house. But it's really for my grandmother to decide," Ben said.

"I want to know if you can see yourself living here, Harry. If not, we'll look at other properties," Lady Philippa said.

At that, Tamsin jumped in. "Ben, what are you looking for in a place to live?"

"I'm not sure. At the moment, my focus is getting my business set up. I need to find the right location for that as a priority."

"You can't continue coming and going from London, Harry, or you will never open your restaurant," said Lady Philippa. "And staying at Gideon's house when you are here is not a solution," she added. "If Sunnybrook Cottage was not rented out, you could of course stay there. As I have said before, I am willing to give the tenants notice to leave, so that you can move in."

"Thank you, Gran, but no. That wouldn't be right. I just need time to think it over."

"What sort of business premises are you looking for, Ben?" asked Tamsin.

"I'm a chef, and I am planning to open an organic farm to table restaurant here in Oxford. I think it's the right place and time for something like that, ideally on the river-bank. So I need to find a building that suits that business, and my vision."

"Is that the River Cherwell, or Isis, or does it matter?" asked Tamsin.

"Either. I know what I want and how it needs to be laid out, but I'm not getting anywhere looking myself."

"I could help you with that, if you like," said Tamsin. She regretted saying it immediately, because it would mean even more travel to Oxford. But she felt she could really help Ben, and any sales would help her. It was clear he was confused about how to find the right property.

"That would be amazing, but I wouldn't want to put you out."

Before Tamsin could reply, Lady Philippa said, "It's

settled then. Tamsin will help you find the right premises for your restaurant, and in the meantime, you need to think about this cottage and if it's a place you can see yourself living in, or if you want something else. Shall we move on?"

Ben and Tamsin looked at each other with surprise at Lady Philippa's conviction and direction to them both and walked to the front door of the cottage.

"If you have time, maybe I could tell you what I'm looking for over a drink at Brown's?" suggested Ben.

"That would be great, but I have to get going. Can you send me an email with your price range, preferred location, wish list and any properties you have considered already? Then we can talk next week."

"Yes, will do. Thanks for showing us the cottage today. It's really nice. I am just focussed on my business as the first step," said Ben.

"I understand," said Tamsin, and then walked back to her car, leaving Ben to join Lady Philippa in her Bentley.

CHAPTER 7

Trying on all of her dresses was making Tamsin extremely stressed, and she poured another glass of Chardonnay to calm her nerves.

Jason had called when she was in Oxford, and left a very strange message saying he needed to see her, tonight.

She had called him back and sent him a message to find out what he wanted, but he didn't reply.

He then texted her an address and time to meet and she was preparing to join him in an hour at a place in Spitalfields they used to go to early on when they were dating.

They'd had many drinks dates there, and several dinners alone and with friends over the three years they were together. She wasn't sure meeting him was a good idea, now that Jason was married and expecting a baby in a few weeks, but she thought that it must be important if he asked her to dinner, last minute, on a Saturday night.

Finally having decided on a bold, body hugging, one shoulder red dress, and then changing her mind several times, she eventually landed on the red dress and black heels and was stepping out the front door when the phone rang. It was her mum.

"Hi mum," she said.

"Tamsin, can you come for dinner tomorrow?" was all her mum said.

And she knew it was a set up to meet one of her parent's friend's sons. He'd likely be visiting his parents for the weekend, and her mum had the idea to invite Tamsin down to Margate to meet him.

"Can't, mum. I have to be in Oxford again on Monday. Early," she said, hoping the lie would not be obvious.

"Oh, ok," said her mum, obviously disappointed.

"What's up though? Is it important?"

"No. It's just these new friends we met at lawn bowls have a son visiting them, and we met him this week at the bowling club. He's a very lovely young man, a dentist from London, and we thought it would be nice for you to meet him. They are all coming over tomorrow for dinner, which we just arranged."

"Oh, sorry, mum. But I really can't. Raincheck?"

"Ok."

"I have to go, mum. Heading out with Becca tonight and I'm running late."

Tamsin felt awful lying, but mentioning Jason would just cause her mum to worry.

"Ok, dear. Have a good time. Talk to you next week."

"Bye, mum."

"Bye."

Feeling horrible about lying to her mum, Tamsin justified doing so because she wouldn't be able to tolerate another blind date. Each of the five her parents had arranged had been disasters. Seeing the cab had arrived, she grabbed her black croc Aspinal evening bag, a gift from Jason on their last Christmas together, and she went outside.

CHAPTER 8

In the cab, Tamsin rubbed her hands together to warm up. She felt cold, having forgotten to take gloves with her. Yet her palms were sweating. She was suddenly very nervous about seeing Jason, who she hadn't seen alone in over a year.

Tamsin wondered what Jason wanted to tell her.

A few minutes into the drive, she almost asked the driver to take her back home, but was far too curious and excited to turn back now. There were lots of things that he might want to say.

Maybe he had changed his mind about the rent, and wasn't going to double it. Jason's father was a reasonable man, and he may have convinced him that it would not be right to squeeze Tamsin out by doubling the rent. She hoped it was that, but it didn't seem likely. Jason could have just called or texted if it was something as simple as that. She figured that whatever he wanted to say had to be something serious, that required them to meet in person.

The cab pulled up to the restaurant on Commercial Road and Tamsin took a moment to breathe deeply before stepping inside the front door of the steakhouse. Hawker's was one of the most popular restaurants in London, with bookings needed months in advance. How Jason had snagged one was a mystery. It was likely his father had the reservation and gave it to him at the last minute. His stepmother Julia was always changing her mind, so it wasn't unusual for Jason to get great theatre or opera tickets or last minute restaurant bookings that belonged to his dad because Julia had lost interest.

"Hi, I'm here for the Parker reservation. Nathan or Jason Parker," she said.

"Please, follow me," said the hostess. "How is your evening so far?" she asked as they started to weave their way through the restaurant.

"Fine. Great. Thanks," said Tamsin, wishing the hostess would stop the small talk so she could think.

She scanned the large dining area and although the light was dim, creating a soft lit romantic glow around the room, she could see Jason seated at a corner table, and her heart beat fast with excitement.

He looked *incredible* and was wearing one of his signature white shirts, open at the neck. His tanned skin glistened and Tamsin remembered how he looked underneath his clothes. His black wavy hair was perfect. He wore navy trousers, handmade brown leather shoes, and his cufflinks reflected the light. He saw her, and his beaming smile, which she loved so much, appeared as he got up to greet her.

He leaned in, brushing his lips on her cheek as he whispered in her ear, "You look amazing," while he touched her elbow and then slowly ran his fingertips down her bare arm before he sat down. She was speechless. He had already ordered champagne, which was open and chilling, and he poured her a glass.

❄ ❄ ❄

"Tams," he said after dinner.

He'd called her Tams. His old nickname for her.

He took her hand, and linked his fingers with hers.

"Tams, you and I were so good together. What happened to us?" he asked.

What happened, she thought to herself, *was that you ran off with your twenty-two year old secretary.*

He had broken her heart, ripped it out of her chest, stomped on it a hundred times, and then threw it in the river. So Jason did not have the right to call her Tams. Not after that.

"I, you, I mean," was all she could say, feeling the soft touch of his hand holding hers and missing him more than she ever had.

"I miss you, Tams. I really need you in my life." He looked at her and she couldn't speak.

She felt the same way about him, but it was hopeless. He was married. He had cheated on her and left her to marry someone else, when they had made plans for a life together. And now, he was about to become a father.

She wondered how he dared to call her, take her to one of their old favourite places, show up looking gorgeous, and then tell her he needed her. It just wasn't fair!

All of a sudden, as if she had been listening to their conversation but not participating, Tamsin snapped out of the fog she was in, moved her hand away from his, and said "Jason, I loved you. Loved you with all my heart. I still love you, even though I don't know why. That's why calling me out here tonight is so cruel. I supported you through the hardest part of your qualification to become a barrister, sacrificing my own needs and my own desires, and you left me. You didn't think about my feelings. Maybe you never loved me at all. How could you, since you ran off with another woman?"

He tried to interrupt but she continued, "You got married, and now you are about to become a father. So it's NOT ok for you to call me up, ask me to dinner, and tell me how much you need me. I can tell that it's all lies anyway, even though I want it to be true. I'm actually ashamed of myself for getting dressed up and coming here tonight to see you. Thank you for dinner, and goodbye."

His face had turned from a seductive, loving look to one of surprise, and then shock.

She reached for her handbag, stood up, turned around and walked away. By the time she got into the cab, Tamsin had three missed calls and messages from Jason, and a missed call from Ben. She silenced her phone, laid her head back on the headrest, closed her eyes and exhaled deeply, desperate to get home and in disbelief of what she had just done.

CHAPTER 9

Sunday 10th November

Having a dessert with Becca at Livori café in Knightsbridge was just the salve Tamsin needed. She'd gone home and cried her eyes out for ten minutes after having dinner with Jason, then made a cup of tea and fell fast asleep.

In the morning, she'd called Becca, and said she needed some BLove. When Tamsin was doing the soothing, they called it TLove. It was a silly term, but they'd used it since they were children and had made it up when things got too hard for Becca, whose parents were always arguing.

Becca and Tamsin had been at school together in Margate for a few years before Becca's father had left them, and her mom moved the family to London. They'd always been best friends, and that would never change.

"What's up, T?" Becca asked when she answered Tamsin's call.

"Meet me at Livori, 11am, before the Harrods crowd shows up."

"K, see you."

"Bye."

"Bye."

✳ ✳ ✳

Tamsin arrived early on purpose, so she had time to stop in at Harrods. She walked the main floor and inhaled all the gorgeous scents. She wanted to see what was new in make-up at her favourite brands. She loved the way Harrod's was laid out, like an organized garden maze at a large country house, where you could get lost and hide and never be found.

Stopping by Chanel, she saw the new Christmas palette, with all the deep, rich colours, and rows of shimmering eye shadows in gold and silver. She quickly fell back to earth because she couldn't afford to buy anything. But even if she could, she had nowhere to show off such incredible make-up.

After a walk around La Prairie and spritzing herself with the new Jo Malone, she realized it was time to leave the wonderland of Harrods and headed out to meet Becca.

✳ ✳ ✳

As she approached the window of Livori, her new favourite café, she spotted Becca in the window. She waved, and walked through the old school turnstile to enter. There were at least thirty cakes on display in the window, enticing anyone with a weakness for sweets to come inside. It was a truly amazing place, with the freshest cakes in London. They were all hand made on site, and Tamsin wanted to try each one.

Becca got up to hug Tamsin, and it was a deep, affectionate hug, like the feeling of a warm duvet on a cold winter night.

"So?" Becca asked with anticipation and understanding, gently pushing Tamsin's hair away from her face, which had been blown around by the wind outside.

Tamsin sat down next to her in the window alcove, and looked at the incredible coffee and slice of cake Becca had ordered for her. It was impossible to decide which dessert to pick, since there were so many options, but Becca knew what she liked. Chocolate raspberry molten lava cake. Delicious.

"I saw Jason last night," Tamsin said.

"You what?!" Becca nearly choked on the bite of cake she had just taken.

"He's been ringing me ever since."

"What are you talking about? Am I in a parallel universe, or what? Explain."

"Ok, well, he texted me yesterday morning, saying he needed to see me urgently, and to meet at Hawker's. Of course, I wondered what he wanted, and the only thing I could think of was that he must have changed his mind about doubling the rent."

"Right. He's such an idiot. What does he think he's doing with that anyway?"

"I don't know. But no, that was not what he wanted. He looked incredible and I was just being stupid even going there to meet him. I was completely floored by how gorgeous he looked, as always, and then he took my hand and said, 'Why did we break up? We were so good together', he needs me, and on and on."

"And? What did you say?"

"I lost it. At first, I was mesmerized, as I always am around him. I wasn't following what he was saying. But then I thought, *wait*, he really *means* this. He is actually sitting here, with me, while he's a married man, with a wife about to have a baby, and he's asking me to give us another chance."

"I can't believe I'm hearing this. Or that you went. What were you thinking, T? And what was he doing? What was he thinking? Or not thinking, as the case obviously was," Becca said, taking another bite of her pistachio cake.

"I don't know. And I don't care, Becca. I told him that was it. We're over. *Forever.* And he's been calling me ever since."

Tamsin went on to tell Becca about the trouble she would be in if she couldn't get the higher rent together starting in January, and the real prospect that when she went home to Margate next month for Christmas, she'd be staying there.

"You can always move in with me, Chris, and the kids. You know that," Becca said.

"Oh, I know. I know. And I love you for it, B, I really do. But I *will* get things sorted. I have to. I've decided that on Monday, I'll take on these two flats in Shoreditch to sell that have just been sitting on the books. And they have to sell, right?"

"Of course. It's Shoreditch," she said.

Shoreditch was one of the hottest spots to be in London. Recently gentrified, but just gritty enough to retain some street cred, saying you lived there was making a statement that you were cool, but also that you had arrived, since it was so expensive. And maybe most important of all, it highlighted that although you could live in a nicer neighbourhood, which might be safer, cleaner and have better schools, Shoreditch was where you chose to be. The prices were out of control, like everywhere in London, so people who lived there were making a statement about their wealth and their interest in being seen.

"I know, right? I should be able to get those flats sold in a week."

They talked about Becca's kids, seven and four, who were both in school now and driving Becca slightly mad. She had a nanny to look after them, since she and Chris both worked full time, and they could afford it. But Becca was born to be a mother and loved spending time with her kids and she spent every minute she could with them. She got on well with the nanny, which was a bonus. This morning Becca had her husband take over child minding, so she could slip away to see Tamsin on the nanny's day off.

"What's going on with all that travel to Oxford? Are you still going up there?"

"I am. There's a cottage there I'm trying to sell, which is really lovely, although very expensive, but it's taking far too long to get rid of. I've had four, no, five offers on it now, and the client has refused every single one."

"So what's the issue?"

"It's the perfect place for Londoners to have a Cotswold weekend escape, but too small for families to live in full time. I'm hoping my American client will buy it. Americans love the idea of the English country cottage. He's made an offer, but the owner hasn't responded in days.

"Because it's small, it limits the pool of people who want to have it. In the past, a family would have lived in it just fine, but it's not big enough for today's families with all their stuff.

"I have a client, Lady Philippa, who wants to buy it for

her grandson, Ben, but he doesn't seem to be very interested in living there, and he's on his own, as far as I can tell.

"I'm going to help him try to find a building to buy for a restaurant, since he's a chef and wants to open one in Oxford."

"Have you got time for that?" asked Becca. "I thought going to Oxford this much was killing you and costing a lot."

"It is, and it does. But right now, it's my best bet to earn some proper income. I will start marketing the Shoreditch flats, and hopefully between these three properties, at least one will sell in the next thirty days, so I can afford to stay where I am. Of course, I'd rather move out of the flat, even if only to mess up Jason's plans, but I don't have the six weeks minimum for a deposit on a new place."

"Do you think Jason is going to let you stay there after last night?"

"I don't know. I don't see why not. It's not like I said anything that wasn't true. He left me. It's over. He thinks he wants me back, but he doesn't. He's probably just panicking about becoming a father, and he wants an escape. I think he might be addicted to ruining his relationships. I almost convinced myself last night that I should give him another chance, but then my brain kicked in and I stopped myself from saying things I might regret."

"Thank God for that."

The waiter came by to see if they wanted anything else. It was getting very busy and there was a massive queue, since it was approaching lunch time. A couple were staring at them, hopeful it would get them to leave. But they each ordered another coffee and a cake to share this time, indulging themselves.

CHAPTER 10

Monday 11th November

On Monday, Tamsin went to see her boss, James. She wanted to tell him that she would take on the two flats to sell, and to update him on Lavender Cottage. She knocked on his office door.

"Come in," he said.

"Hello, James."

"Tamsin. What's happening with Lavender Cottage?" he asked. He leaned back in his chair, and clasped his hands behind his head, as if he were settling in for a story.

"Well, as you know, sir..."

She wondered why she always called him sir when she was nervous. He'd told her to call him James but sometimes she would just get tongue tied and make a mistake.

His office smelled of a cologne that he had custom made, and it was very strong. Tamsin felt it was overpowering, and sometimes got a migraine if James was in the office all day. But he didn't seem to notice the impact of it on her. Every day he wore a different scent, and all the bespoke fragrances he had invested in must cost a small fortune.

She tried to focus her thoughts. "The cottage has had

four offers, as you know, and on Saturday I presented another one to Mr. Crighton."

"Yes, he told me."

"And, although all of these offers have been good, in fact, you could say great, considering one was at the asking price, for some reason, Mr. Crighton has not accepted any of them. It's as though he is not ready to sell the cottage. I wanted to talk to you about it to see if there is something I am not aware of that is holding him back."

"Not that I know of. He said this latest offer meant it would not complete until May, and that irritated him."

"I know, but the client just can't take the cottage until then. It does feel like he's being inflexible."

"I'll talk to Cyril. Otherwise, is all well?"

"Yes, everything is fine. I wanted to let you know that I will start working on selling the two flats in Shoreditch."

"That's good. I'm not sure what the issue is with those. They should have sold by now."

"I'll do my best. Is there anything else?"

"No. You can take Sammy with you on any showings for the flats on Sclater Street. He's starting today. Maybe he can make some calls for you to organize some showings."

"Thank you, James!"

Tamsin was overwhelmed at this gesture. Offering the support of a new member of the team to Tamsin was either a sign of respect for her hard work and dedication, or a last attempt to help her sell something, because she was still on probation and that was running out at the end of the year.

Worrying about whether she would pass that and still have a job in January was just too much to think about on top of everything else going on. She closed the door behind her and looked for Sammy.

"Lily, do you know where Sammy is?" she asked the receptionist.

"He's over there, by the photocopier."

Tamsin walked over to talk to Sammy, introduced herself and asked him to start making up brochures and sending them to people in the database who were looking for flats for sale in Shoreditch up to nine hundred thousand pounds, which would be the right type of buyers.

CHAPTER 11

At lunch time, Tamsin looked at her phone, which was still cracked. She had an email from Ben, and five missed called from Jason, as well as voice messages.

She listened to the voice messages, all of which were from Jason, as she suspected they would be. The first two from Saturday night were him asking her to come back into the restaurant. The third was about an hour later, once he'd realized she wasn't coming back, and he asked her to call him. The last two had been sent on Sunday and had a more resigned tone, his voice sounding like he'd accepted what she had said, but still not believing she had said it.

The email from Ben was long, with a list of all the buildings he liked in Oxford, including two he had seen, listed by a local agent. He hadn't liked either of those, which he considered to be too small.

Helping him was going to be a challenge, she thought. His budget was large, but availability was the issue. All spaces of the necessary size on or near the river were occupied by successful businesses, except for three buildings. And only one of those was for sale. The two others seemed to be abandoned. She'd get back to him later, she thought. Now was the time to focus on London and getting to work on selling the flats.

❄ ❄ ❄

By one o'clock, Sammy had sent Tamsin a list of five people in their database who had indicated interest in flats like the ones they had for sale in Shoreditch. She called them all and left messages.

The two flats were side by side and located in a large converted warehouse. Each of them had floor to ceiling windows and exposed brick walls. The building was located on Sclater Street, just far enough from the Shoreditch train station to be quiet, but within a short walk of the high street. The flats were ideal for singles, couples or possibly families who wanted to live in an edgy neighbourhood and could afford it. She would love one herself.

It had been a long and difficult weekend and Tamsin was tired. She had to stay focussed, but she was getting worn down. Dinner with Jason had exhausted her. She had never been that tough with anyone before, and she liked how it made her feel. Saying what she meant and sticking to it would be difficult if she saw him again, so she would have to avoid him.

As she walked along Kings Road looking for a place to buy lunch, she thought about how Jason was the best looking man Tamsin had ever been out with. After Saturday, she had been trying not to think too much about their relationship, or him. They had enjoyed three years of living together, quite happily, and she still didn't understand why he had left her. What had she done, if anything, to lose him? Everyone had told her the answer was simple. She had done nothing wrong. It was Jason's choice to deceive her, and he had done that for at least a year.

When they had split up, all of their friends had taken sides. Most of their friends were Jason's, so she'd lost contact with almost all of the people they had spent their time with. Jason hadn't really ever warmed to Tamsin's friends, and they were all glad that he was out of her life, especially Nico and Andrew, who both seemed to see right through his lies. From the start, they both had doubts about Jason's intentions towards Tamsin and felt that he was using her. They tried to share that with her as kindly as they could, but Tamsin didn't listen to them.

Worrying about how things had ended, and why, was a colossal waste of time. Jason knew just how to break down Tamsin's defenses, and he had tried very hard to do that at Hawker's. Avoiding him at all costs, no matter what, would be essential from now on. It was only a few weeks until the rent would double, she'd move out, and then she'd never have to talk to or hear about him again.

When she got back to the office, she sat at her desk and thought about Becca's reaction when Tamsin told her she had seen Jason on Saturday night. Having cake and spending time with Becca had been fun and she realized that she missed her a lot. They didn't see each other as much as they wanted to anymore, although it was understandable. Becca was a brand manager with a global company and a mum of two little ones, so they did their best to get together when they could.

Tamsin's friend Andrew was always there if she needed help or support and she felt guilty now that she'd called Becca instead of him to natter on about Jason, but her relationship with Becca was different to the one she had with Andrew. He was fun to go out with on a Saturday night for drinks or dinner, but not the best help when it came to talking about her love life.

Andrew loved to have a good time, not settle down, so he was not best suited to give relationship advice. Tamsin and Andrew had met when she joined a gallery in Soho, where Andrew also worked. Now he was a curator at a museum. He had done very well professionally, although his love life was all over the place. He travelled a lot, and she missed seeing him.

When it came to Jason, Tamsin needed Becca to help sort her feelings out. Or sometimes she would lean on Nico. Next to Becca, Nico was Tamsin's oldest and closest friend, who she had worked in a part-time job with at university. He always told her the unvarnished truth, in a nice way.

Becca knew how confused Tamsin could be about Jason. She had never liked him, from the very first time they met. Becca had tried to convince Tamsin that Jason wasn't right for her, but she never listened to anyone's advice about her and Jason's relationship.

She was smitten with him from their first date, and, looking back, she could see the early warning signs that he was not trustworthy, but she had ignored them. She would not make that mistake again.

Sometimes it seemed that everyone else's life was moving miles ahead of hers, achieving their professional and personal goals and dreams, while she was going back-wards. Her love life was non-existent and her work, and income, were precarious. But she had determined to turn it all around and these new flats were the key.

CHAPTER 12

Tamsin took the train to Shoreditch and ordered a coffee from a place she hadn't been to before. It was probably new, she thought. The area was constantly re-inventing itself with new businesses. She passed all the usual places, like Beigel World, the chocolate shop and a few tattoo artists and hairstylists. She noticed a new vegan cheese shop as well. Everyone was rushing around, and the streets were buzzing with the hustle and bustle of a typical London weekday. Even Mondays were very busy in Shoreditch.

As she entered the building and took the lift to the flats, she was impressed. Everything looked good. The main entrance was clean, and the fact the lift was working was a great sign that the building was being looked after properly. All these things mattered to buyers.

When she opened the door to 5B, she was surprised by the amount of daylight pouring in through the windows. The flat was flooded with sunshine, and the exposed brick walls were the softest colour of tawny brown, making the place feel warm and ready to be lived in.

The flat next door, 5C, was exactly the same. Gorgeous. And they were both empty, which meant they could be sold faster. She texted Sammy some thoughts of things to add to the online listing and her phone rang while doing so, from a number she didn't recognize.

"Tamsin Davies," she said.

"Tams, it's me," said Jason.

She waited a moment before speaking, while she gathered her thoughts.

"Jason, I have said all that I'm going to say to you. I will be out of the flat by the end of the year, and I'll leave the keys in the kitchen. If there is anything else you have to say about the flat, let me know. Otherwise, please don't call me again. Goodbye," she said and hung up.

He called back twice, but she let it ring to voice mail. She considered blocking his number but realized that was unnecessary, since she would be free of him soon.

When she got back to the office, Sammy said that two people had called wanting to see the flats. One was a DJ from Liverpool, who was driving down to London and wanted to see them later that afternoon.

"Ok," said Tamsin, not wanting to travel all the way back to the flats, but excited there was some interest. People wanting to see the flats this fast was more than she could have hoped for. "Why the hurry on his end?"

"He said he's a cash buyer and is looking for a place in London. He needs somewhere in time for his New Year's Eve party. The venue he was going to use has cancelled his booking to take a wedding instead."

"New Year's Eve party? It's not likely he can get the place in time for that."

"I did explain that to him, but he was very persistent. He offered to waive some checks in order to have the place by December fifteenth, if it looks as good in person as it does in the photos. He actually said he wants to see both flats, so I went ahead and booked him in for later today. I looked him up and he's a big deal up in Liverpool."

"Ok then, let's go over there now, so we are there a little before he arrives. I want some time for us to walk around the block and see what's new in the area. I didn't have time to do much of that earlier. You can help me talk the neighbourhood up. I assume you know a few places you can mention in Shoreditch, if he asks?"

"Yes," said Sammy, "I practically live there at the weekend."

At three o'clock, Antony Verona Cabello, aka Antony V, as he was known professionally, showed up at the building on Sclater Street, more than thirty minutes late. He stepped out of the back door of a Mercedes with blacked out windows, wearing an enormous gold chain and jogging pants.

Tamsin worried that being late was a sign he wasn't serious, but she tried to keep an open mind, considering he had come all the way from Liverpool. Trying to tell his age, but generally being rubbish at guessing that properly, Tamsin thought he couldn't be more than twenty-five years old. She resolved to check out the DJ online later, and kicked herself for not doing it before now.

The office admin team had pre-qualified him as a cash buyer, and had verified he had the funds available, so she showed him the flats.

"Hello, I'm Tamsin. And this is Sammy."
They all shook hands.

"Antony."

"My colleague, Sammy, said you would like to see both flats, for a quick purchase, in order to hold a New Year's Party. Is that right?"

"Yeah," he said in a very pronounced Scouse accent.

When they entered 5B, he walked around, and then asked "Can I knock this through?" while tapping on the common wall between the flats.

"I don't know," Tamsin said. "We could find out."

"That would be best. I need a big space here in London, and these two flats opened up together as one would do it."

"You could make confirming that a condition to be agreed with your offer." She was being pushy now, but he seemed very keen. "Do you like the flats?" she asked.

"Yes, they could work," he said, although he seemed to be pondering whether they really would work or not. "Are there any people here likely to give me agro over the odd party?"

"I don't know. I mean, you can generally have guests over. I think it just depends if it's getting out of control in terms of noise. What is it that you have in mind?"

"Nothing much. Just a small event on New Year's Eve where I'll be hosting a live televised countdown."

"I see. I'm sure that wouldn't be a problem, as long as any permits are applied for."

Tamsin had no idea what would be required to have television crews in the flats for a live broadcast, but that was well outside her domain. She wanted to shift the discussion on to whether he would like to buy them or not.

They left the flats with an agreement that she would make an offer on his behalf for both flats at one million eight hundred thousand pounds, the asking price, to secure them both.

He didn't want to buy only one. Since the flats were both empty, she was hopeful the deals could be done on time.

"Well, that was easy!" said Sammy as they left and Tamsin locked the door of the second flat.

"It's not done yet," said Tamsin, being cautious. "Let's go call both sets of owners to make the offers and see what they say. I don't know if they will want to do what's needed to get these sales completed by December fifteenth, which he was pretty clear is a deal breaker if we can't do it."

"Yeah, everyone is getting focussed on Christmas now. Does that mean people are less likely to be looking and wanting to buy properties at this time every year?" Sammy asked.

Sammy was brand new to real estate and just out of college, so Tamsin felt she should help him understand the real estate buying cycles and talked him through that on the way back to the office.

CHAPTER 13

When Sammy and Tamsin walked back into the office, Lily said, "Bad news. Your buyer for Lavender Cottage, a Mr. Herrington from New York, has said he's taking back his offer."

"What?! Why? It hasn't been declined. Mr. Crighton hasn't said yes to the offer, but he also hasn't said no. I need to ring him right away and find out what he thinks."

"Here's the number for Mr. Herrington." Tamsin went to her desk and put her headphones in. She walked to the kitchen to get a coffee, while calling the seller of Lavender Cottage to find out if he was going to accept the last offer that had been made, or not. She tried three times, but could not reach him, so she sent him a text asking him to call her and left a voice mail message.

Then she called the buyer, Mr. David Herrington, to find out what the issue was and why he had said he wanted to rescind his offer on Lavender Cottage.

"Hello?" a male voice she didn't recognize said.

"Hello, is that David Herrington?"

"One sec," a young man with an American voice said as he handed the phone over to someone else.

"David here," said the now familiar voice of her buyer.

"Hello, Mr. Herrington. This is Tamsin Davies. I have

been out and had a message that you rang, asking me to call back."

"Yes. Listen, has the seller accepted my offer? I have found a better place for my daughter, so if he doesn't want to sell the cottage to me, then I'm going to make an offer on the other one."

"Right," Tamsin started to panic. "What is this other property, Mr. Herrington?"

"What? What's that got to do with anything?" he asked.

"Well, I'm happy to talk through the features of that other house with you and see how it compares to Lavender Cottage, while I continue trying to reach Mr. Crighton for an answer. I have called him and left a message saying that it's urgent he call me."

"What is wrong with him? You can't just leave people hanging like this. It's been days since I made the offer."

"I know, and I understand. Buying a house is a different process here to the US, as you are aware. So, it can take a little longer to agree than you might be used to." She thought this sounded reasonable and hoped he would understand that the way they did things in London was not the same as in New York.

"I'll give it to five pm today," he said. "I'm still in the UK, so that's local time. If he hasn't accepted my offer by five, you can consider it cancelled."

"I will do everything I can to reach him right away, and hope to have his acceptance by then. I will get back to you soon," Tamsin said. But she knew deep down that the sale was not going to happen. Mr. Crighton had left his response too long, and now the buyer didn't trust him.

"Tamsin?" asked Sammy, as soon as she had hung up.

"Yes?" she asked as she turned around to face him.

"Ben Smythe-Jones is downstairs, asking if you are here."

Why would Ben be here, in London? she wondered. She then remembered that he had a place in Kensington.

"Are you free to talk to him?" Sammy asked.

"Yes, take him up to Albert Bridge."

Tamsin was not in the mood for talking to Ben at this moment.

She wanted to find a quiet place to scream.

The most critical deal that she'd had a chance of completing since starting at Red Brick Realty was hanging in the balance. She didn't have time for Ben Smythe-Jones right now.

Trying to calm herself down and furious that the biggest deal she had going was about to fall apart, she'd have to find a way to get rid of Ben nicely, but quickly, and keep chasing Mr. Crighton.

She left him a message explaining that the offer on Lavender Cottage would be null and void if he did not accept it by five o'clock because the buyer had found another house. And she dropped James a note as well, asking him to do whatever he could to reach Mr. Crighton.

CHAPTER 14

Each meeting room at the office had been named after a London bridge, and she walked past several before coming to the right one. Ben was already seated, and someone had served him a coffee with two Christmas biscuits.

"Ben, nice to see you," Tamsin said, as she sat down across from him, calm and collected as she could be, given the circumstances. "What brings you to my office?"

"Hi, Tamsin, sorry to come here unannounced, but I was just at my place and thought that since I hadn't heard from you, I'd drop by and see if you were free to discuss my property search."

"I am in the middle of a couple of things right now, but did you not get my email?" Tamsin now wondered if she had sent the email she'd written to Ben, given what was happening on the weekend and how busy she had been today.

"No, when did you send it?"

"Um," and she thought about when it could have been. "Saturday evening, just before seven?"

"Nope. Nothing here from you yet," Ben said as he checked his phone.

"Ok. Well, sorry about that. I have a deadline of five o'clock today and need to deal with that and something else right now. Can we..." and he cut her off, suggesting they meet later.

"How about meeting after that? We could go for a drink at the bar downstairs and talk then. What do you think?" he asked.

She wasn't keen on talking to clients after hours, and wanted to get home for a long soak in the bath. Her plans to have one on the weekend after returning from Oxford had been turned upside down, and she had been looking forward to having one tonight. Given that Ben had made the effort to show up at her office, and hadn't received her email, she agreed.

"I could meet you at six. In the meantime, I'll try to find the missing email and re-send it."

"Sounds like a good plan," said Ben, standing up to leave. "See you down there at six."

"Thanks, Ben. See you then."

She walked him to the front door of the office and went back to her desk. Tamsin knew the place he meant was The Orchid, a new bistro downstairs on the ground floor of the building. It would be quiet on a Monday evening, so they would be able to talk.

Clicking through her sent items, she couldn't find the email she was sure she had written. It had taken time to write, so she was becoming irritated she couldn't find it. Eventually, she found it stuck in the draft folder. She remembered that she had planned to add a third property to it before going to meet Jason on Saturday night, and then her mum had called and she'd forgotten all about it.

She looked again at what was for sale in Oxford that was either a restaurant right now, had been previously or could be converted to one. Since Ben wanted something on the river, the prices were high and the options were limited.

There were two empty commercial properties which would be very expensive to fix, but since Ben had over five million pounds available to buy something and refurbish it, either of these could work.

Both places looked charming, and each had two storeys. One had Edwardian architectural features and the other, Art Deco.

Neither building had been used for a very long time, judging from the information she could find online. That meant a lot of work would need to be done, if the layout of either could even work for a restaurant.

Technically, Tamsin shouldn't be doing commercial real estate work. She was a residential agent and there were two other people in the office who normally handled commercial deals. But the search for a restaurant building had fallen into her lap by accident. She hadn't found time yet to tell James what she was up to and she hoped he wouldn't mind. Since he was the owner of the agency, he had the final say on what they sold and who they helped.

Tamsin didn't fancy having to keep going to Oxford, which she would need to do if she was going to help Ben look at places, but it was good experience taking on a commercial buyer, and the commissions were much higher.

She'd need to get a fee agreement in place with Ben before she did any more work helping him search. She'd discuss it with him tonight, and check with James before doing the paperwork, if she saw him.

She looked on Google maps to see what other restaurants were located nearby the two disused buildings. She searched for farm to table or organic eateries, but there weren't any right on the river, or within walking distance, so that was a good sign.

Tamsin emailed the addresses of the two empty buildings to Ben, along with her questions for him and her ideas about how to approach buying a commercial property in Oxford.

Only one of the buildings was for sale, so it would be easy to get in to see that one. But since the other one was not, it could turn into a time consuming exercise for Tamsin. She would first have to find out who owned it, and and then convince them to sell it, or at least let her look at it with Ben.

She looked at the time and turned her attention back to the other properties she was dealing with. James came over and stood by her desk while she finished a call with Antony V. When she hung up, he said, "Cyril Crighton has told me exactly what he told you. He will accept the offer from your US buyer, but he cannot wait until May. Can you call David Herrington to see what flexibility he has on the date? Asking our seller to wait six months for his property sale to complete, when the buyer is ready with cash right now, and can conclude the sale in a matter of weeks, makes no sense to him. Or to me, frankly."

"I will do, but he was adamant that he is unwilling to take the cottage until his daughter starts university. She was going to start in April, but now it's going to be July, and he thinks he's compromising by agreeing to complete in May."

CHAPTER 15

By four-thirty in the afternoon, the cottage offer had fallen apart and only one of the sellers of the two Shoreditch flats had accepted the offer from Antony V. Tamsin had forgotten to ask James about the right commission percentage to charge for helping buyers with commercial real estate, and now he had left and Lily said he was not available for the rest of the day. She'd have to go with what she'd come up with, a three percent commission.

She couldn't believe how obstinate Mr. Crighton had been about the date to complete the sale on Lavender Cottage and she had tried everything to convince him to sell it to Mr. Herrington, since her livelihood depended on selling something in the next six weeks. But when he said he wasn't willing to wait more than the usual period to complete the transaction, she had to give the bad news to David Herrington, and he had walked away, furious with her, the agency and the whole process.

Putting her own anger aside, and desperate to get home to scream into a pillow, she tried to focus. The only prospective buyer Tamsin had left for Lavender Cottage was Lady Philippa. She'd try to find out more later from Ben about how interested he and his grandmother were in the cottage. Talking to Ben in person about it would be better than a call, during which she could be more easily brushed off and the cottage rejected.

Tamsin had a headache from the busy stressful day she was having and went to get another coffee, although she knew it might make it worse. Sometimes caffeine helped her when she had a headache but it could also keep her up at night. Given she still had a busy evening ahead, she took the chance.

At six o'clock, headache gone, Tamsin packed her bag, and headed downstairs to the very beautiful Orchid wine bar and bistro. It was owned by a French couple and had only been open for three months. Tamsin had not been there before and was impressed by the décor when she walked in. It had the feel of a Parisian speak easy, or at least what she thought that would look like, with lots of mirrors, ornate black chandeliers and a very long bar with mahogany tables and chairs with blue velvet seats.

It might have been better to meet at the pub on the corner, she thought. The Orchid seemed more like a place to go for a date or romantic drink. But since she was here now, she ordered a large dry white wine, and had a seat in a booth. She opened her bag and took out all the details for the two empty buildings, the contract she needed Ben to sign, and some other information on his restaurant competition, as she understood it. To be fair, she didn't really know much about what type of food Ben was going to sell, or who his target clientele would be, but she had a good idea. It was likely to be tourists and well-heeled locals, the usual type who would be looking for organic, local food, and willing to pay a lot for it. All she needed to know was whether the restaurant was going to be vegan, vegetarian or serve fish and meat. That would help her clarify Ben's competitors, which she hoped he already knew, and ensure she directed the search properly, avoiding buildings close to any other restaurants that served similar food. She was sure that Ben would not want to open his place near a restaurant of a similar type and she felt she should look into what was in town already and what might be in planning permission, although technically, these things were not part of her job as an estate agent. Hopefully, he'd see this as excellent service, and not question her commission figure. On a two million pound purchase, three percent would net her, well, a lot of money, even after the agency took their cut of the commission. And the one building currently for sale wanted much more than two million pounds.

As Ben walked in, she didn't recognize him immediately. The bar was filling up, and she was quite far in the back. When he got closer, she saw his blond hair first, then noticed he had changed into trousers, a blazer, and a dress shirt. Earlier he had been wearing jeans and trainers.

Extremely handsome.

"Hi, Tamsin," he said.

"Hi, Ben."

"Thanks so much for meeting me last minute like this," he said and leaned in to kiss her on the cheek.

Smells fabulous.

"Not at all. I'm happy to."

And now she was glad she had agreed to meet Ben, and

felt she'd been a bit harsh ushering him out of the office earlier, even though she did have a deadline.

"Alright!" he said and clapped his hands together. "I see you have just ordered, so I'll be right back. Can I get you anything else?"

"No thank you. I'm fine for now," she said.

Ben came back with a glass of red wine.

"What did you order?" she asked.

"Château Lafite," he said, and she thought how pricey that was.

"Ok," said Tamsin as she put all of the paperwork on the table between them, eager to get down to business. "What I have here is what I emailed you earlier, and sorry that didn't get through the first time. I had meant to send it on Saturday before I went out in the evening and was sure I had."

"Did you go somewhere nice?"

"Uh, yes. Hawker's."

"Which one?"

"On Commercial Road."

"I was there last night. We could have run into each other, since my plans were originally for Saturday."

What a disaster it would have been to see him there, she thought to herself.

She quickly changed the subject, worried he would ask who she had gone there with.

"I need you to sign a buyer agreement, Ben, and I suggest a finder's fee of three percent, if that is good with you."

"Yes, that's fine."

"I have found two empty and essentially abandoned buildings, which might work. Both on the river, and one of them is for sale. So, if you are interested, I suggest we start with that one. But first, can you tell me more about your restaurant? What type of food are you going to serve? When do you want to open? And what type of space are you looking for?"

Ben had sent her a reply, which she had briefly reviewed before he arrived, but she wanted to get the details from him and discussing this in person now would save a lot of time later.

He explained that most of the day to day activity would be overseen by his friend Giles, who would be the sous chef. Ben would be the head chef, coming up with the menus, doing the public relations and directing the marketing. It was his face and name that would generate the business, at least at first.

"My vision is to have a beautiful and functional space. It's taken me a long time to get this far – much to my grandmother's chagrin – since she is funding most of this for me, and has been waiting years for me to take the crucial step of opening my own restaurant."

Ben wanted to serve up to fifty people at one time, have two plated servings an evening, and provide a lunch service six days a week. Oxford was busy enough in the town centre to warrant a daily lunch service. He said that while it might be considered ambitious by some to think that a new restaurant could fill two timed seatings for dinner and also run a lunch service right from the beginning, Ben was confident that through his family connections, the restaurant would be full every day, and ideally have a long wait list.

Tamsin wasn't sure about that, but since she knew

nothing about restaurants, she listened intently to what he said.

"So, what you want is a space with two floors, room for fifty people to dine at the same time, and a long bar; something like this," she said, pointing at the bar beside them.

"That's right."

"And when are you planning to open?"

"April. We have just under five months to get things up and running so we can open during Easter break."

Tamsin didn't know anything about opening or running a restaurant, but it seemed that many things would have to be timed perfectly, including the purchase and closing on the property, to make Ben's timeline work.

"Are there any special features or requirements that I should be aware of?"

"Not really. I mean, I am likely to strip back any place to the core, and re-build the entire interior, unless there are some unique attributes I want to keep, like cornices or chandeliers. Much of what I do with the space will be decided once I have secured the right building. Then I'll bring in my architects and designers."

"Well," she asked, after they looked at photos of the buildings, "Do you like the potential of these two empty spaces?"

"They look great."

"Should I call the agent of the one for sale and try to locate the owner of the other one so we can get in to see them both?"

"That would be ideal," said Ben.

He seemed to go along with every suggestion Tamsin made, which normally she'd be excited about, but it made her nervous. He could just be enthusiastic, but she suspected he was very inexperienced at buying property, and had already said this was his first restaurant. She worried that he could say yes to things that may turn out to be a 'no' once Lady P got involved. It was clear she was making the final call.

"And just to be clear, the funds are in your account now, and are rightly, legally, yours?" she asked, needing to confirm this.

"Yes, my grandmother has gifted me five million pounds to buy a building, and to bring it up to the appropriate standard necessary."

"Alright then. I'll get on with this tomorrow," she said, as he signed the contract and she put the papers away.

Her phone rang, and she excused herself.

When she returned, she found Ben had ordered more drinks for them.

"I got you a Sauvignon Blanc. Hope that's ok," said Ben.

"Cheers, and thank you."

"Are you hungry?" Ben asked.

"Famished. Yes." Tamsin hadn't eaten all day and was now aware of that.

"Fancy trying a vegetarian Italian restaurant nearby?" he asked. "My friend is part owner, and it's really good."

"Let's do it," said Tamsin, curious to try something new and ready to eat and relax.

After finishing their wine, they walked to the restaurant, called Silvio's.

CHAPTER 16

"Mister Ben!" They were greeted by Silvio Cosenza, who owned the restaurant with Ben's friend Peter. Silvio had landed on hard times during Covid, and needed an investor to stay open. Peter had been a customer for many years and suggested he could invest in the restaurant. That saved Silvio from bankruptcy and Ben took as many of his friends and contacts there as he could.

"Silvio, hello!" said Ben as he leaned in and they hugged one another heartily. "This is my friend Tamsin."

"Oh, Bella Bella! How nice to meet you! Come in!" he said as he ushered them in. The restaurant was busy, but there were two tables free and he sat them at the one in a quiet corner. Tamsin didn't know it, but this was called the Chef's Table, which Ben explained during dinner was a special table that most restaurants kept aside, should friends of the chef appear at any given time.

Silvio's Restaurant was the type of place that you still found in pockets of London, mostly Marylebone, or Knightsbridge, where they used linen tablecloths and napkins and created the right setting for a meal, whether it was a business meeting, a romantic dinner or a family celebration.

Tamsin was impressed with what she saw and hoped

the food would be good. The lighting was low and the wine was delicious.

"What is this again?" Tamsin asked of the wine she had been poured.

"It's the house white. Which is crazy, really, since it's an incredible vintage of Pinot Grigio."

Intrigued by the idea of a vegetarian Italian restaurant, and not knowing what to expect, Tamsin was pleasantly surprised to see how imaginative the dishes being served to those around her were. Landing on a vegan lasagna, she couldn't wait to try it and the flourless vegan chocolate cake for dessert.

Tamsin had said yes to dinner because she truly was hungry, but she hadn't expected this type of intimate setting. A candle flickered on the table and the lighting was very low, appearing to have been turned down just after they were seated. Feeling like this was no longer a business meeting but a date, she asked Ben what type of food he would be making at his new restaurant, trying to keep the discussion professional.

"Mostly vegetarian, although I'd love it to be a fully vegan restaurant. There are a lot of options in vegetarian cooking, because you can use some animal products, like dairy. With vegan food, options are more limited, although the flavours and food are just as delicious. You have to be more creative with vegan food. It takes some planning, and sourcing organic food is more difficult still, especially at scale, so a restaurant with one hundred plates a night, plus a daily lunch, is big enough. Maybe too big, but I want to go all in, now that I am ready for the challenge of having my own kitchen. Running what I hope will be a Michelin starred restaurant means I will need to continuously innovate the menu and I'll be better able to do that if it's primarily vegetarian and not vegan."

"What made you interested in vegetarian and vegan cooking in the first place?"

"I don't know. I get asked that a lot. I started to reduce the amount of meat I ate when I was at university, and then I felt I didn't need it. It had just been a habit to always have meat or fish. When I'd go home from university, I'd be overwhelmed by the volume of food and the variety of meat my father has served every day. I had never noticed that when I was younger."

"Are you from Oxford originally then?"

"Yes. My father is the Eighth Earl of Tansley, and eventually, I will be the Ninth. I grew up in Tansley Hall, and went to Oxford University."

Tamsin was surprised to hear that Ben was a member of the aristocracy, but didn't want to seem inquisitive about that. She assumed that Lady Philippa must have been married to a Lord, but didn't really understand the ins and outs of the peerage and wasn't sure if Ben was a Lord, or a Viscount, or a Duke, or something else.

"What did you study there?"

"Law."

Law. They already had something meaningful in common, she thought.

"How did you become a chef?"

"About five years ago, I just decided I'd had enough of the city. I had been working in a brokerage as a trader, and of course the money is very good and I really enjoyed the work, but I wanted something more meaningful to do every day. So I looked into the Cordon Vert cooking school in Cheshire and did some classes there, to see if being a chef might be right for me. I loved what I learned there, and have not looked back. I then worked in Paris for a few years to pay my dues and learn how to run a kitchen and now I'm ready for my own."

"Sounds amazing to change careers like that. I guess I've done the same, really."

"Tell me more," said Ben, as he tucked into the bread and olive oil, while they waited for their starters.

Tamsin went on to explain that her degree in Art History had led to a good job, but that circumstances meant she'd needed to earn more and now she was in real estate.

"Do you like it?" Ben asked.

Tamsin thought for a moment before replying. "Yes, I do. It's interesting finding out what people like and do not like about houses, and learning how people choose and then use their living spaces."

"The cottage you have in Oxford is really nice."

"It is! Have you thought any more about whether you want to buy it?"

"I have. I think if we can find the right building for my restaurant before Christmas, then yes, if it's still for sale, I could make an offer. Or Granny can. Either way, I think it's worth having. The kitchen has been remodeled very nicely, but there are still some refurbishments to do there."

"I know."

The main dishes arrived and the presentation was beautiful. There were edible flowers on the lasagna and it was delicious. Ben had ordered the same dish as Tamsin, saying that he had a weakness for lasagna. Tamsin didn't want to reveal her weakness for chocolate cake, or all things sweet.

They ordered a second glass of wine each, she drinking white and he having red, and they chatted about lots of different things.

When they left the restaurant, Ben hailed Tamsin a cab, and paid the driver for her journey. She was surprised by his generosity and thanked him as she got into the car.

"I'll call you tomorrow once I've spoken to the agent representing the building for sale, and ideally having found the owner of the other building as well."

"Great stuff, Tamsin. Thank you. Safe journey and see you soon."

"Thank you for dinner, Ben. Goodnight," said Tamsin and the taxi drove away.

❄ ❄ ❄

Reflecting on the delicious meal she'd just had, and feeling a little bit tipsy, Tamsin wondered if dinner with Ben had been a date, and if he'd planned that all along, showing up at her office unannounced mid-afternoon, or whether it was nothing more than a business meeting with a client. She wasn't sure.

He'd asked her to have a drink at Brown's when they'd met at the cottage on Saturday, and he'd also asked her to see him again the first time they had met, by chance, at the Poacher's Den, and each time she had declined, although for good reasons. She hadn't really considered that he might be interested in her, but tonight there seemed to be a spark between them.

Ben was very good looking. Not in the way that Jason

was, who had model perfect looks, and all heads turned in his direction when he entered a room, but Ben was really attractive. She'd now seen him in both a laid-back rural look, at the pub, with jeans and wellies, and today in a more formal environment, wearing smart clothes. He was blond, and she didn't generally find herself attracted to blonds, but there was something about him that she really liked.

He was charming, friendly, respectful, and genuine. At least that was her reading of him based on what she knew so far. But she had been fooled before and now was not the time to start dating anyone new. Not with uni about to start and her financial worries taking up so much of her energy in order to make them go away.

It would be fun to help Ben find a space for his new restaurant, and now that he had told her about his plans in more detail, she was excited to do it, even though it meant more travel to Oxford. Ben had also been very positive about Lavender Cottage, saying that he might make an offer on it before the end of the year, which was what she needed. Since all the other offers on the cottage had been turned down by her very fickle seller and she didn't know what he would accept, she'd made a mental note to get advice from James on what would motivate Mr. Crighton, because he'd known him for years.

The cab arrived at her flat and she went inside, changed out of her work clothes and into some comfy night clothes, and fell asleep.

CHAPTER 17

Tuesday 12th November

Tamsin woke to a loud banging noise. She was half asleep but was sure it was her front door. She snuggled in further under her duvet and tried to ignore it, but then she heard Jason's voice.

"Tamsin, please let me in."

Is he serious, coming here so early in the morning?

She got up and put a robe on, then walked to the front door and looked through the spyhole to see if it was in fact Jason.

It was, so she opened the door, but left the chain on.

"What, Jason?"

"Can you let me in, please?"

"Why? What do you want?

"I just need to talk to you."

"It's seven in the morning on a workday. I need to get ready and out of here soon."

"Won't take a minute, I promise."

She thought about it for a second, knowing that whatever he had to say, she'd regret letting him in.

"Okay, but hurry up," she said, and unlatched the door.

He came in and sat down on the couch.

"New things. I like it," he said, looking around and noticing the lamps her mum had brought by recently. He'd comfortably set himself on the couch, with his arms stretched out over the back.

"What do you want, Jason?" Tamsin asked, standing in her robe and slippers.

"Tams, it's like I said. I really need you."

"She's kicked you out, is that it?"

"No," he said with feigned shock she would suggest such a thing.

Tamsin waited, arms crossed.

"Well, sort of," he said.

"I knew it. Ok, out please, Jason. I have to get to work. I told you already, I'll be gone by Christmas and you can have the flat back. Until then, I need you to leave me alone."

"Can't I just flop here until then?"

"No! Of course not. Go to your father's place. Anyway, when is your baby due? You need to sort things out with your wife, Jason."

Saying all of this was hard, since she still loved him. He could always manipulate her feelings when she saw him in person, but she held her ground.

"Please, go home. You can move in here when I go to my parents for Christmas, if that's what you need. It's only weeks away now."

Sheepishly, he got off the couch, trying his best to make Tamsin feel sorry for him by looking as pathetic as possible. He made a sad, poor me look that she could normally not resist, but Tamsin wasn't going to let any of Jason's old behaviors sway her. He left and she made coffee, proud of herself for how she'd handled things, and got ready for work.

❄ ❄ ❄

By eleven o'clock, after several attempts, Tamsin finally reached the estate agent of the building for sale on the river in Oxford. She had learned a lot about the property, which she looked forward to sharing with Ben, and had the other agent's availability for times and days that she and Ben could see it.

The owner lived in America and was selling his UK assets, so he was open to offers. The listing price was two million, eight hundred and fifty thousand pounds. Tamsin didn't have enough experience with commercial buildings to know if that was the right price, but it would be somewhere over two million five hundred, in her estimation.

The other building Ben wanted to explore was owned by a trust of some sort, but Tamsin hadn't been able to find out how to contact them. Since that one was not for sale, it would be harder to get contact information or find out more, but she'd keep trying.

Pleased with her progress, she popped out for a coffee and a pastry, and thought about what had happened earlier that morning. She could not believe Jason's behaviour.

Did he still think that after two years apart, she'd take him back?

And now he was a husband and would soon be a father.

He must be really struggling.

A pang of guilt came across her, but Tamsin did not know why. She wondered just for a moment if she had done the right thing by telling him to go.

He'd seemed distraught at first, but Tamsin felt he'd fooled her about that, so she would let him come in. He must think she was still unable to resist his charms, even though they hadn't been together for ages.

He had options. He could go to his father's house and stay there if things were not working out with his wife.

At the moment, she really didn't care.

Tamsin's thoughts turned to her parents and having Christmas with them. She would have to talk to them, soon, and tell them what was going on. Her rent being doubled meant she would have to find a new place to live in the next couple of weeks, or move back home.

It was outrageous that Jason wanted to charge her so much more for rent, when he knew she couldn't pay it. He was being completely heartless. He would never get that amount if he put it on the open rental market, so how he would get his six bedroom house, Tamsin did not know. But she reminded herself that she just didn't need to care anymore about anything Jason was doing.

She was starting to look forward to moving out of the flat. It had always felt like Jason's and not hers, or even theirs, no matter how many of her own things she had added to it. This might be just what she needed, leaving the flat. If only she had funds for a deposit on a new one, she wouldn't be feeling so stressed about it all.

CHAPTER 18

For the rest of the afternoon, Tamsin tried to get hold of Ben, but wasn't able to. She was disappointed, since she wanted to book the showing of the empty building.

At six o'clock she packed up, went home and decided to call her parents.

"Mum?" she said when her mother picked up the phone.

"Hello, dear!" Her mother sounded busy, which was unusual.

"Mum, I'm going to have to stay a while when I come home for Christmas."

She had finally said it.

"What's happened?" her mother asked, with curiosity and concern.

"Jason is doubling the rent, so that he can buy a house in Sevenoaks for his wife and new baby."

"I see. Can he do that? Hasn't the new government put in a law preventing this type of thing? Your father was telling me about it the other day."

"Yes, but it's not in effect yet, so he can raise the rent, and as much as he wants. Even if I could afford to pay it though, it's not worth that amount. Besides, staying in his flat does not make sense anymore. We broke up a long time ago and I need to move out and get my own place."

"Your father will be over the moon if you come home and live with us."

"Just don't tell him yet, ok? There is still a chance I may be able to get a different flat and move there instead. I wouldn't want to get dad's hopes up."

"If you come home, will you be able to go back to university?" her mother asked, hopeful the answer was yes.

"Maybe. I don't know, mum. I have to think. Right now, I have to sell some properties, so that is what I'm focussed on. Even living with you and dad, I'd still have tuition to pay, and it's thousands of pounds every term. And I still have to pay the loan for my undergrad degree as well."

"Ok, dear. We have the Millers over for dinner, so I need to go now. I'll not tell your father anything until you decide what to do, but call us if you need help making any decisions. We love you, dear."

"Love you too, mum. Say hi to dad, and to the Millers for me."

"Bye-bye."

"Bye, mum."

❄ ❄ ❄

Tamsin watched some reality television, while digging around in the cupboards for something to eat. She hadn't done a shop in a while, and there wasn't much food in the house. Settling on some tinned soup and a tuna sandwich, she ate and then logged on to her computer to see what other buildings might have come up for Ben to consider. He hadn't been in touch all day, and she wondered why.

The owners of the first flat in Shoreditch had accepted the offer from Antony V by email just before she sat down to eat, and now she saw an email from the sellers of the second flat, saying they wanted more money than they had been offered.

It was a very cheeky move, thought Tamsin, as Antony had offered the sellers their asking price. They went into some detail about how it was risky for them to get into a deal and be dependent on another seller, so she asked them what price they wanted and they replied with a figure. But they still would not commit, even when she asked them if they would if she got them their new price. She'd just have to tell Antony he'd need to pay more to get their agreement. Realizing this could wait until the morning, and feeling very sleepy, she headed to bed.

CHAPTER 19

Wednesday 13th November

It was a cold morning, with frost on the ground. Tamsin had left without checking the weather, which was a mistake, because now she was freezing. She desperately needed a scarf and gloves, both of which she'd left at home, and regretted not taking with her.

As she waited at a zebra crossing, a man stepped out of the back of a Rolls Royce and into Boots. Tamsin thought to herself that if she had a car like that with a chauffeur, she'd also pay someone to go to the pharmacy, rather than do it herself.

There was so much wealth in the area where she worked that sometimes she forgot it wasn't how most people lived. The people she interacted with at work were all well off, but her own situation was precarious and needed to be sorted out fast. Being evicted, which was really what was happening by Jason doubling the rent, was a terrible feeling, but she knew she could go home to her parents' house if she really had to.

The priority now was to sell both of the Shoreditch flats, which had to be sold together, and the cottage in Oxford, while also finding Ben a restaurant to buy. If she could not pull these sales off, there would be no way she could study law. And her dream of becoming a barrister would truly be over.

At nine-thirty Ben called. "Tamsin, so sorry I didn't get back to you yesterday," he said, rather breathless. "My step-mother broke her arm and I had to take her to A&E."

"Sorry to hear that, Ben. Is she ok?"

"Yes, but she is furious. Pepper is a keen equestrian and this is a real blow to her lifestyle. She rides every day for at least two hours on the estate. But never mind that. I got your email and the building sounds brilliant. When can we see it?"

He was referring to the one for sale, which was the only one she had been able to get information about.

"How about tomorrow? I had them agree to hold some times for us tomorrow as well as on Friday. I can pick up the keys at the agency in Oxford, and meet you there."

"Of course. What time?"

"They have one o'clock or later in the day."

"How about one, and then if you have time, we could grab a coffee or lunch and talk things through?"

"Alright, I'll meet you at the building at one and in the meantime, I'll keep trying to get the details for the other building."

"Sounds great, Tamsin. Thanks so much and see you then. Oh, WAIT!" he said, having forgotten something. "I'm in London right now, so we could go up to Oxford together tomorrow," he suggested.

"Um," said Tamsin, not sure this was appropriate. Given their relationship was professional, she should be doing the driving, and she really didn't want to take him in her tiny old car. He'd be used to much grander vehicles and she had already seen him in a Bentley.

"It's ok if you'd rather not," he said, sensing her hesitancy.

"No, that's perfectly fine!" she said, but not feeling it.

"I can drive, if you don't mind that arrangement?" suggested Ben.

Then as if he could read her mind, which focussed now on how she would get back to London after the appointment, he said, "I could drop you at Oxford Station once we are done, and you could take the train back to London. Or, I could drive you back to London on Friday. You could stay at Tansley Hall tomorrow night if you like."

No. No. No.

Tamsin started to panic.

This was all too much, thought Tamsin.

Ben was a client, so it was *her* job to take *him* around if there had to be any driving done together. But really, she should just meet him wherever they needed to be. She definitely should *not* go in *his* car or stay at his father's *house*!

Quickly trying to come up with an alternative, she said, "I can ride up there with you, and then you can just drop me back at Oxford for the three o'clock train back to Paddington," she said firmly and with certainty that this was the right way to handle things.

"Ok. Perfect plan. See you then, Tams. I mean, Tamsin. Sorry, didn't mean to be over familiar there," said Ben.

"It's ok," said Tamsin, although it didn't feel ok. Being called Tams only reminded her of Jason, and he was the last person she wanted to think about.

CHAPTER 20

Close to five o'clock, Antony V called back. He was not happy about the situation, but said he would pay an additional hundred thousand pounds for the second flat. Since the sellers of the first flat were aware of the higher price their next door neighbours had negotiated, they now wanted the same price as well. So he reluctantly agreed to that too.

When she got off the phone, Tamsin had to pinch herself. She had just sold two flats in the space of a week, for *two million pounds*. The agency would get a commission of one and a half percent, of which she would receive a portion, so there was going to be more than enough money to secure a new flat.

But could she get one before Christmas?

She would not be paid until January for the sales of the flats, unless she managed to get an advance. That seemed unlikely, because the sales may not go through, and was why everyone was paid after a sale was completed. She'd ask James, just in case. And probably today, since other people might have the same idea to ask for pay advances, with it coming up to Christmas.

Antony V needed both flats by December fifteenth for his New Year's Eve Party, or he would not proceed with the purchase. Getting this settled on time would be her only priority now. She called on Sammy to help.

"Sammy?" Tamsin called him on WhatsApp.

"Oh hey, Tamsin, I'm just on my way back from helping Sarah at her client's house in Tooting."

"Great. Great," she said, not listening. "Because guess what?" she asked, not waiting for a reply. "We've sold the Shoreditch flats!"

"What?!" said Sammy.

"That's right. We did it!"

"*You* did it," he said. "You are truly amazing at this, Tamsin."

"Thanks, Sammy. Now we have to get moving so that these sales really happen. When you get back to the office, let me show you all the legal things to get Antony V started on. There is a lot to do, and I need you to work beside him every day to get it all done on time."

"Ok, will do," Sammy said. "I'm really chuffed for you, Tamsin. This is such great news."

CHAPTER 21

Thursday 14th November

In the morning, Tamsin worked from home until eleven, when Ben picked her up. When she got into the car, she smelled coffee and in the console saw that he had brought her a latte and a croissant.

As Ben had a brand new Mercedes, with a tan leather interior, Tamsin was petrified to eat or drink in Ben's car, but when he noticed that she hadn't touched her coffee after fifteen minutes, he said with a smile, "Go on and enjoy your coffee and croissant. I'll clean up any crumbs later."

Tamsin very much doubted that Ben would be hoovering the car, but she was hungry, so she tucked in, trying to keep the croissant half in the bag while munching on it, so as not to make a mess.

On the way, they stopped for petrol, and when they got out for a few moments, Ben looked at her, and, reaching out his hand to wipe something off her cheek, he smiled and said, "Little croissant flake there, Tamsin."

She was mortified.

"Hehe," she laughed, self-consciously. "Thanks, Ben," was all she could come up with.

She turned away from him as he went inside to pay,

and vigorously wiped off her lips and both cheeks, in case there was anything else on her face, then checked how she looked in the car's wing mirror.

After a short stop, they continued on and found the drive wasn't too busy, surprisingly. When they got to Oxford, they drove straight to the building they were scheduled to see.

The light from the river was reflecting off the front window and the stained glass pane in the top half of the door was creating a kaleidoscope of colour across the empty floor. The building really was magnificent. It needed a lot of work, which they could tell from the outside, but it would be a gorgeous restaurant if it was refurbished properly.

"The listing agent has decided not to come with us," said Tamsin, after checking a new text that had come in.

"So, let's go get the keys and come back and see it ourselves."

They walked up the road to the office of the listing estate agents, retrieved the keys and then strolled back to the building along the river. It was very busy now, being lunch time.

Tamsin tried the key, and it opened the latch, but the door was stuck and there were piles of mail to push through on the floor to get the door open.

Not very professional, Tamsin thought. The agent could have picked up the mail knowing they were coming.

Once she got the door open, and Ben had pushed the mail aside, they walked in, looked up, and stood, speechless. The second floor had a balustrade, with a railing that ran in a semi-circle around a wide staircase. There was a circular staircase in the centre of the room that wound up to the first floor. The roof was a glass dome, with moss growing on it and many leaves, but once cleared up, it would be glorious.

Tamsin was also taken by the beauty of the space. She looked at Ben and he turned to her and said, "This is the place."

CHAPTER 22

Tamsin had been trying to obtain the contact details for the owners of the other building and once she did, had called them several times. They were now finally calling back.

"Hello, Tamsin Davies," she said as she answered her phone. "Yes, that's brilliant. As it happens, we're here now, if that works for you?"

Hanging up, Tamsin told Ben that the owner of the other property, which was only two doors away, had no plans to sell, but would be willing to show them the space. He was on his way over now. Tamsin locked up the building and went two doors down with Ben to see the second property.

"Wow! This one is amazing as well," she said as they approached the front door.

"Yes, let's see what it looks like inside," said Ben.

"Hello. I'm Alfred Cummings," said the man who Tamsin had just been talking to on the phone as he approached them on the street.

"Tamsin," she said, holding out her hand to shake his.

"Ben," he said, doing the same.

"This property has been in my family for a few generations. It's been used over the years for a lot of different purposes, but never as a restaurant."

He opened the door and they entered. It smelled very

damp. The plaster on the walls was peeling off and there were cracks on the walls. Tamsin wondered why it was sitting empty and how long it had been like this.

As if he anticipated the question, Alfred said, "We have not been able to agree as a family what to do with this building. It has sat idle for over thirty years, which is when my mother inherited it from an uncle. My siblings and I were all living abroad and raising our families at the time, so none of us bothered to think about it. We all know it's worth a lot, but I'd have to convince both my brother and my sister to agree to sell it, and I don't know how easy that would be. My brother lives in the US and is in a care home, with dementia, so we would have to pursue power of attorney. If you think you would like to lease or buy the building, we could discuss it further."

The situation sounded very complicated, so Tamsin hoped that Ben preferred the other building. So far, it looked to be in much better condition, and it was for sale.

"Ben, take a look around and I'll wait for you here," Tamsin said, while he wandered off to check the floor above.

After about ten minutes, Ben returned, having looked thoroughly at the building. He seemed ready to go.

"Thank you very much, Mr. Cummings," said Tamsin. "Showing us your building has been very much appreciated. Ben and I will be looking at a few more properties and will get back to you soon."

After saying goodbye, it was obvious Ben had not fallen for this place in the way he had for the first one. They walked back to the front of the other building, and he asked if they could go inside again.

"Yes, let's do that," Tamsin said and opened the door.

❄ ❄ ❄

"Here you could put a long bar, a really long one, so the drinks could all be prepared here, and upstairs there is also room for a second bar, and there is even a dumb waiter!" Ben was so excited he couldn't stop telling Tamsin how he thought the place could be laid out.

Tamsin listened to all his plans, smiling because his enthusiasm for the place was contagious.

"And I would put a fountain here in the middle. Something really tasteful. In keeping with the period when this place was last updated, the nineteen twenties or early thirties. Look at all the Art Deco details that are still here," he said, pointing to the ceiling.

"Take a look at this amazing fireplace! A wood burning fireplace right in the middle of my restaurant, in a building that's at least two hundred years old! I couldn't have asked for more than this."

Ben was imagining all sorts of ways the restaurant could be laid out and Tamsin could see his mind coming up with lots of great ideas. It was obvious he wanted to get started on refurbishments immediately.

"Can we go get something to eat and talk this through?" Ben asked Tamsin.

"Absolutely. Let's go."

"Brown's?"

"Yes."

They walked the twenty minutes or so to the world famous Brown's.

CHAPTER 23

Once they had ordered a drink, Tamsin asked, "Well, what do you think about the buildings we have just seen?"

"The second place is not right. It's just, I don't know. A feeling I have. But the first one is amazing. I can see it. I can actually see my vision coming to life in that space. It's perfect."

They settled into the comfortable red leather seats of the booth and moved closer together to look at the listing online, including the photos. It really was an extraordinary building, and had a rooftop patio with views of the river, as well as two floors indoors, just as Ben had requested. There was so much he could do with the space and his ideas were overflowing. Even Tamsin was getting excited by the way Ben explained what would go where.

Their legs touched and Ben said "Excuse me," and moved away just far enough so it wouldn't happen again, but their hands were almost touching on the table.

"I need to get Gran in to see it."

"Ok," said Tamsin, slightly confused.

She had understood that Ben had control of the funds to buy a building. Maybe he just needed his grandmother's approval before he spent the money she had given him.

But maybe she hadn't given it to him yet, and getting it required her approval.

"Let me call her right now," he said.

Dessert arrived, and Tamsin had sticky toffee pudding. Next to molten lava chocolate cake, and crème brûlée, this was her other favourite. Ben stepped away from the table when his grandmother answered his call, and when he came back, Tamsin was tucking into the vanilla ice cream. She was on a sugar high.

"Any chance we can go back and see it again today? Gran is at Tansley Hall. She has agreed to come down if we wait for her."

It was now after four o'clock and Tamsin had missed her train to London, and given the keys back to the estate agents on the way to the restaurant. She called them but there was no answer.

"Let me try them again in a minute and see if we can go back in today."

"If not, can you stay over and we can go in the morning?" Ben asked.

Tamsin wasn't expecting that. She didn't have anything with her, so staying over was not ideal.

"You can stay at Tansley Hall. We have everything you could possibly need there, so don't worry about not having anything with you. I'll call Gran back and tell her it's ok, she doesn't need to come to town now."

Ben was so excited about the place and she didn't want to dampen his enthusiasm, so Tamsin agreed. Tamsin would have preferred to check into a B&B if she had to spend the night, rather than stay at Ben's house, but she thought it would be rude to decline the offer.

She called the estate agent again and this time they answered. She made arrangements for her, Ben and Lady Philippa to see the building again at ten o'clock the next day. It would be better in the morning than it would be now, since it would be dark by the time they got back to the building, and a place like that had to be seen in the daylight.

She called Sammy to make sure things were moving along with Antony V, and the sale of the flats, which they were. When she hung up, she realized she had forgotten to ask James if she could have an advance on the commission for the Shoreditch flats. She'd have to do that tomorrow, when she got back to the office. And she still hadn't asked him if it was ok for her to help a client buy commercial real estate and what commission percentage she should charge. Tomorrow, for sure, she would get his time. In the meantime, she planned on spending the evening looking for flats and calling her mum to tell her that she wouldn't have to move back to Margate after all, now that she had sold two fantastic properties.

CHAPTER 24

As they drove up the long drive to Tansley Hall, Tamsin couldn't see anything but trees. Then, all of a sudden, the Hall appeared, but was still half a mile away. The size and scale were like nothing she had ever seen before. They were only a few miles outside of Oxford, but it was so rural, it seemed like they were the only people around for miles. When they pulled up in front of the Hall, a man appeared immediately, and welcomed Ben home. He took the car keys, while someone else opened the car door for Tamsin, and she got out.

"Thank you," she said to the man.

It was dusk, and would soon be dark, but with the remaining daylight, she could see fields and hills stretching as far as the horizon. *Could the Smythe-Jones own all of this?* she wondered.

"After you," said Ben to Tamsin as he held out his hand towards the front entrance.

There was music playing when they stepped inside the grand entrance to the Hall. Piano. A woman appeared, stopped and looked at them. Tamsin thought it must have been her playing the instrument, and on hearing them, she had come into the front entrance hall to the grand residence.

"Ben, who is this?" said the woman, with a hint of irritation in her voice.

"Pepper, this is Tamsin, my estate agent. Tamsin, this is Pepper, my step-mother."

"How do you do?" Pepper said, without moving forward to shake hands.

"Very well, thank you," said Tamsin. "This is a lovely home."

Pepper nodded her head very slightly, as if agreeing and dismissing her at the same time.

"Tamsin will be staying the night," said Ben.

Pepper's eyebrows slightly rose, and Tamsin could tell she was surprised by this.

A man appeared out of nowhere and asked if there were any bags. Ben said no and asked Tamsin to go with someone else who had silently appeared by her side, a woman in a maid's uniform.

"Ma'am," she said.

"Hello," Tamsin said, not quite sure what to do or how to refer to her.

The woman began walking, so Tamsin followed. They took the stairs to the first floor and then walked down a long corridor with many doors on both the right and the left. After what felt like a long walk, the woman opened a door, and stood aside, so Tamsin could enter first.

"This is the Marlowe Suite."

Having a suite to herself, Tamsin started to think that getting stuck in Oxford for the night might not be so bad after all.

"My name is Helen, and I will be assisting you while you stay at Tansley Hall. A robe, slippers and toiletries can all be found in the en suite," she said, walking towards and pointing to another large room to the right.

Tamsin was relieved to hear it, since she had nothing with her.

"You will find multiple pillows and additional blankets in here," Helen said as she opened a floor to ceiling wardrobe with mirrors. "Dinner is at nine. Do you have anything to wear?" she asked.

Tamsin wondered why she'd need to wear something other than what she had on to eat dinner.

"No. But I've just eaten. I won't need to have dinner."

Tamsin realized from the look on Helen's face that she had broken an unwritten rule by suggesting she would skip the evening meal.

"I mean, I would be happy to join."

Helen visibly cringed.

"I mean, it would be lovely to have dinner with Ben and his family this evening. But no, I do not have a change of clothes."

"Lady Tansley will have something you can wear. I will make enquiries," Helen said and left.

Tamsin thought this was all a bit much, even if they were Lords and Ladies and this was an ancestral home.

Surely in the year 2024 people do not dress up for dinner at home.

But apparently so, she realized, when, ten minutes later, Helen arrived with three incredible dresses, gloves and wraps to choose from, along with matching shoes, all of which looked brand new. As she was looking at them, Ben appeared in the bedroom doorway.

"I see you are settling in," he said, leaning on the

doorframe. "Shall I show you around, and introduce you to my father?"

"Yes, sounds good," said Tamsin, wanting to leave the decision about what to wear to dinner until later. She wasn't sure whether she should leave at this particular moment, since Helen had just laid all the items out for her, but then Helen bowed and left the room, as if respecting some sort of code. Tamsin wondered, was she supposed to be doing a curtsey to Ben? Was he a Royal? She had no idea what the protocol was.

As they walked through the Hall, Tamsin realized that the house was incredible and wished she had looked it up online when Ben had told her where he lived.

Clearly, this was an ancestral home of tremendous significance. There were extensive gardens, fountains, stables, and over seventy thousand acres, with farmland growing many different crops. There were several cottages, two hundred tenants and the family had their own chapel. They didn't have time to see much of the estate, but Ben explained how it was laid out and showed it to her on a map.

"Father?" Ben said as he knocked on a heavy wooden closed door.

"Come," came the reply.

As he opened the door, Ben said, "Father, this is Tamsin Davies. She is helping Gran and I with the restaurant."

"Very good. Nice to meet you, Tamsin," Ben's father said, while getting up from behind an enormous desk. He came and stood in front of it, leaning back into the desk. Tamsin felt he was trying to assess her before she even spoke, and she thought she would not stack up.

"Hello, Lord Tansley," she said, hoping that was the right greeting and kicking herself for not having asked Ben what to call his father. She assumed this was right since no one corrected her.

"To what do we owe the pleasure of your company?" he asked. She wasn't sure if he was genuine about it being a pleasure to meet her or if he might be using sarcasm. It was impossible to tell from the way he said it.

Ben chimed in. "We have just seen the most incredible space for my restaurant. Granny will come with us in the morning to see it as well. Since Tamsin lives in Chelsea, and I drove us here from London, I suggested she stay here tonight rather than go back to the city, only to come up again early tomorrow morning."

Tamsin had opened her mouth to correct Ben and say she lived in Hammersmith, not Chelsea, but the moment had passed.

"A sound plan," his father said and moved back behind his desk, picking up his glasses. "I shall see you at dinner," he said. And with that, Tamsin felt they had been dismissed.

Ben turned and it was obvious they had been, so they continued their walk through the Hall.

"Is your grandmother here?" she asked.

"No. But she will be for dinner. Speaking of dinner, don't you need to try on the clothes to see what fits?"

"Yes, I do. I didn't realize we'd be eating again, or that we would need to be dressed for dinner."

"Oh, don't feel the need to eat too much if you are not hungry. It's more a ritual than anything. We always have dinner at nine o'clock, no matter who is here."

"Ok," Tamsin said as she returned to her room. *Could this really be how they eat every night?*

"Come down for a cocktail at eight, if you like," Ben said.

Tamsin returned to the Marlowe Suite and had a look at all the items they made available for guests. It was astonishing. She figured that they must have clothes and shoes in every size, not knowing who would arrive unexpectedly. But how did they know what size she would be, she wondered, after trying on each dress and set of shoes and finding they all fit perfectly. The dresses were very elaborate, with beautiful fabrics, but way over the top for dinner, in her opinion. They were suited for a wedding or a debutante ball, if those things still happened. She had no idea. She worried she'd spill something on whichever dress she chose, so she would have to be extremely careful. Who knew what they would be eating? What if it was something she didn't like? This was Tamsin's worst nightmare, being stuck with strangers, in a situation she hadn't planned. She was feeling far out of her comfort zone. She chose the most demure outfit she could, and decided to call her mum.

"Hi mum. I've got some great news."

Tamsin could not wait to tell her mum that not only had she sold two properties in one day, but she had sold them for more than the asking price. The best news was that this would give her the freedom to move to a new flat.

Before calling her mum, she decided to try James on his mobile, just in case he answered, and got hold of him on his way out to dinner. He was in a good mood, thankfully, and agreed to let Tamsin have an advance for the flats. She wouldn't get it for a while, so she'd still need to borrow some money to get a rental deposit together on time to move by Christmas, but Becca would help her with that. She made a mental note to call her in the morning.

"Oh," said her mum, clearly disappointed but trying to hide it, when she told her she would not be moving back in.

"You didn't tell dad I was moving home, did you?"

"No. But I was getting very excited about having you home. I'm happy for you, of course, so great job, Tamsin."

Tamsin knew her mum was truly happy for her but deeply disappointed at the same time. By now, she would have deep cleaned and tidied up Tamsin's old room, even though it was always spotless and perfect. She would probably have bought some things to make the space a bit more grown up, anticipating Tamsin's return.

"Do you have a new flat picked out yet?" her mum asked.

"No. I'm going to start looking tonight. I just had to sort a few things out at work first," she said, thinking of the advance.

"Where are you planning to move to? Will you stay in Hammersmith?"

"I don't know. I think it's time to change neighbourhoods, but I'm not sure yet. Maybe Angel or Islington. Somewhere close to work would be ideal, but I can't afford that."

"Let us know if we can help with anything dear."

"Will do, and thanks, mum. Say hi to dad."

"Love you."

"Love you too."

CHAPTER 25

Tamsin decided it was time to get into the gown she had picked out, and go down for cocktails.

When Ben said eight, did he mean eight, or should she be early, or slightly later than that?

She had no idea, so she planned to go downstairs at five past eight.

She stepped into the dress, which was magenta, with a round neck with short sleeves. She tried to zip it up, but it would not close. After a few tries, and starting to sweat, she decided to peek her head out of the room and see if there was anyone around who could help. Not finding anyone in the corridor, she called Ben to ask for help.

When he picked up, she said, "Ben, can you..." and she was interrupted by a knock on the door. "Hang on, there is someone at the door."

As if Helen had read her mind, she appeared to help Tamsin.

"Oh, never mind, Ben, see you soon," she said and hung up.

Standing with the gown half on, Helen looked Tamsin up and down and said, "Ma'am. I was just coming back to help you dress for the evening."

Tamsin felt quite inadequate at this moment.

Who knew she'd need and have *help* getting *dressed*?

"Thank you, Helen," she said.

Helen helped her get into the gown properly and did it up for Tamsin. She had also brought some jewellery with her this time.

"Would you prefer pearls or diamonds?" Helen asked.

Tamsin's mouth dropped open when Helen presented two cases bearing jewelled necklaces and earrings.

In front of her were two of the most beautiful things she had ever seen. In one box was a three tiered diamond choker, with matching earrings, and in the other, a pearl necklace with matching pearl and diamond studs. These weren't round pearls. They were all different sizes and shapes, so Tamsin thought they must be extra special.

"I couldn't, really. It's not necessary," said Tamsin, uncomfortable with the idea of wearing such expensive clothes and now jewellery as well.

"As you wish," said Helen. "However, the diamonds go particularly well with the magenta gown, and are a natural pair."

"Of course," said Tamsin, realizing that it must have seemed rude for her to decline to wear such fabulous jewels.

"Shall I?" asked Helen, who picked up the diamond choker to assist Tamsin with putting it on.

"Yes," said Tamsin, deciding to give in to whatever rituals were expected of her as a guest at the fabulous Tansley Hall.

Now running quite late, it being eight fifteen, she decided to hurry downstairs to join Ben for the cocktails.

"Helen, where am I going for the drinks?" she asked, now starting to feel more at ease having help while at the same time feeling nervous about dinner and lost in the enormous house.

"Follow me, Ma'am."

Tamsin had also been given a Launer evening bag, which she knew had been a favourite brand of Her Majesty Queen Elizabeth II. She put her lipstick, debit card and keys inside. It didn't fit a phone, or her purse.

She looked good. She knew that. Even though Tamsin was technically average weight and average height, she had always felt tall, and self-conscious about being the tallest woman around. She was often taller than several men at any gathering. Adding heels this evening made her feel even more exposed. But she looked good, and the clothes and jewels would make anyone feel great. The fabric of the dress was comfortable, which surprised Tamsin, and the shoes fit like a glove. There had been gloves for each dress but they seemed a bit much, as this whole evening did.

All this dressing up felt quite pretentious to Tamsin, but clearly this was how they did things *every day* at Tansley Hall. Ben had said as much. Helen was helpful, but clearly didn't think much of Tamsin. It was obvious she did not encounter people of Tamsin's class very often as guests at the Hall.

How strange it must be to have a job serving wealthy people in this way, thought Tamsin. But she had heard about very exclusive butler training in London that uber wealthy people hired all their staff from. In fact, she'd read that the demand was very high for properly trained butlers. She supposed that people with extreme wealth needed something to spend it on, so why not an entire staff of people to look after your every need? Celebrities in America had help, so why not all super rich people, like Ben and his family? If she were honest, she'd probably have staff herself, if she had the means.

As she walked down the main staircase of the Hall, all she could think about was how not to trip and fall. She made it down safely, walking slowing behind Helen, and followed her into a room Ben had not shown her when they had walked around earlier. It was large, but also cozy. There was a piano, and there were several places to sit, although everyone was standing.

"Tamsin," said Lady Philippa, as she entered the room.

"Hello, Lady Philippa," said Tamsin. "How are you this evening?"

"Well, well. Harry tells me he's found 'The one'."

Tamsin was confused.

Which 'one' was Lady Phillippa referring to?

Did Ben have a new girlfriend?

Seeing the confusion on her face, Lady Philippa elaborated.

"The restaurant? On the river?"

"Oh yes! Of course!" Tamsin said, flushing red with embarrassment for not knowing immediatcly what Lady Philippa had been talking about. "It seems to have most of what he is looking for, and I know he's excited for you to see it tomorrow."

"As am I. If I'm going to invest that much in a new property, I want to make sure it's a sound investment."

Now Tamsin really wasn't sure who was buying the restaurant and if it was Lady Philippa or Ben she should be working with, so she thought she'd ask.

"Lady Philippa, will all paperwork for any purchase be signed by you, or by Ben?"

"By me, dear. Harry will be gifted the property by a trust."

Tamsin had no experience of dealing with trusts, so she would try to find out more later, once they were at offer stage.

Ben walked in, came over and leaned in to give both his grandmother and Tamsin a kiss on the cheek.

He smelled great and looked gorgeous. She hadn't really noticed before just quite how attractive he was physically. More than attractive.

He looked sexy.

"Hi, Ben," she said.

"Hello, Tamsin. Who was at the door?"

"Helen."

"Oh yes, just coming to help you dress for dinner, I imagine?"

"Yes."

"Do you have everything you need?"

"Yes. Thank you."

Tamsin wondered what else anyone could need. It felt like every wish could be granted here.

A server in a tuxedo came by with a tray of drinks as Ben went to see his father.

"What are they?" she asked.

He explained what he had, and she took a margarita. Tamsin had assumed there would be champagne.

"Margarita," Ben said when he returned. "I thought you might be more inclined towards a G and T."

"No, champagne usually for drinks events."

"Pepper does not allow champagne. She says it's common."

"I see," said Tamsin, wondering what else Pepper would think is common if even the best champagne in the world was not good enough to serve at Tansley Hall.

Ben's father Charles walked in, followed closely by Pepper. Tamsin wondered if that was her given name or if it was something else. She'd have to ask Ben later.

"Hello, sir. Lord and Lady Tansley," Tamsin corrected herself, realizing she'd jumbled up the greeting by starting with sir.

"Tamsin, you look lovely," said Lord Tansley and this time she could tell his words were genuine. "Everything going well here? Helen is looking after you properly?"

Tamsin was embarrassed to think that Helen's job was to look after her, but she said, "Yes, thank you," and stopped short of saying 'Sir' or 'My Lord', not knowing how to address him after already greeting him.

Did the second greeting revert to sir?

She had read somewhere how to address the aristocracy, but now she could not remember. It had been in one of her historical fiction books based on Tudor times.

"Dinner is served," said someone she had not seen before.

At that, they all made their way to the dining room. Tamsin did not know where she was supposed to sit, but a man in a tuxedo pulled out a chair and indicated that was where she should sit. It was a surreal experience for her. The table was long enough to hold at least twenty people, and she was sitting alone on one side of the table, facing Ben and Lady Philippa, while Lord and Lady Tansley were seated at each end.

The waiter or server, she had no idea what role the person had or even what his name was, came by and served her food. She turned to the right without seeing him and almost knocked a tray right out of his hand. Luckily, no one had seen, so she just pretended it hadn't happened, while worrying again that she might ruin the dress.

They were having chateaubriand, samphire and some small potatoes for dinner, with red wine, which she didn't like. Seeing Pepper put her hand over the glass, she realized that was the signal to refuse a drink, but it was too late. She noticed that no one spoke to the man serving them. They all seemed to just expect he would give them only as much food as they wanted, no more and no less. She'd know this for next time, if she ever happened to be invited back to Tansley Hall, which at the moment, she highly doubted.

After eating everything on her plate, but noticing others had not, she was tremendously full. Lord Tansley said he'd be retiring to the drawing room, and, assuming that was a male-only domain, having read far too many historical novels about grand houses, she had no idea where to go and had resolved to go back to her room and get out of the dress as soon as possible.

As her chair was pulled out for her, she stood up and Ben asked if she'd like to have a nightcap. Wanting to but feeling far too full and uncomfortable with all the food, she declined and headed to her room. Helen was waiting at her door, opened it and helped her out of the dress. She thanked her and said goodnight.

Tamsin logged on to her computer and checked her email, before falling asleep on top of the bed. She woke up in the night, washed her face and got under the covers, thinking how magnificent the bed was. In no time, she fell fast asleep.

CHAPTER 26

Friday 15th November

Tamsin woke up to the sound of Helen's voice, saying "Good morning, Ma'am," as she opened the curtains and let the light in.

Tamsin hadn't even noticed when she'd returned to the room the night before that a bath had been drawn, which had gone to waste, the curtains had been closed and the flowers had been replaced. There were two small marzipan treats left next to the vase and a card announcing when breakfast would be served.

"It's a sunny day. Will you be riding, Ma'am?" asked Helen.

"No, Helen," said Tamsin, who had never been near a horse.

"Are you taking breakfast downstairs?" she asked.

"Yes," said Tamsin, but not sure what to expect when she got there. Her memory from watching Downton Abbey told her breakfast was not in fact served, but self-serve in a house like this. She'd find out shortly.

Tamsin had a shower, dressed in her clothes from the day before, and went downstairs. As she walked into the breakfast room, she saw that only Ben was there.

"Morning, Tamsin. How was your sleep?" asked Ben, as he continued eating.

"Great, thank you, Ben," she said as she sat down at the beautiful oak table.

"Help yourself," said Ben, as he gestured to the side board where an abundance of food for breakfast was laid out.

Tamsin took a plate, added cheese and salmon, yogurt and fruit, then poured a hot coffee and sat down.

"Did you enjoy dinner last evening?"

"Yes, it was delicious," said Tamsin, not wanting to let on how full she had been, or that she hadn't understood she needed to alert the server when enough food had been put on her plate.

"A lot of food. I noticed you finished everything you had been given. Hopefully you were that hungry."

"Not really, but I didn't want to be rude and leave anything behind."

Ben laughed. "It's ok. Daniel knows how much each of us like to eat, but it can be a bit difficult when guests are dining, since he doesn't know your appetite and will keep serving unless you stop him. Feel free to just hold a hand out next time, once you have all you want on your plate."

She wondered if there might be a next time. If so, she must not have embarrassed herself as much as she thought she had. Maybe she'd be invited back, but surely there would be no reason for that. It was strange having a butler, which is what it turned out Daniel's role was, and a Lady's maid serving her, which was Helen's role, but quite nice to be pampered. Helen was not warm, but she was kind and could see this was all new to Tamsin.

"I'm really excited for Granny to see the building today," said Ben.

"Yes, it's a nice day, so hopefully she will get the same feeling we did, with all the sunlight pouring in. Tell me more about your plans for the restaurant, Ben, and where does Giles come into the purchase?"

"Good question. Giles won't be involved in choosing the venue, deciding the layout, or organizing the building works needed to make it into a restaurant. But as a chef, and since he will be the sous chef, he's very keen on helping shape the menus. I know we need to move quickly for an April opening, so if Gran likes the space, which I am sure she will, we can hopefully get an offer in this morning before you go back to London. What is the soonest I could get the keys?"

"That depends on the lawyers, I'm afraid, Ben. Have you instructed one to help you on the purchase?"

"Not yet, but we'll be using William and Tiller, in town. They do all of Father's legal work regarding property conveyancing."

"Once we have agreed on a price with the seller, I'd suggest you call your lawyers immediately and let them know your timeline and how you expect to use the building. They will need to check zoning is appropriate for the building to be used as a restaurant and will advise how many people can be on site at once and other things you will need to know."

"What if there is an issue with usage permission?"

"Then your lawyers will advise you what the process is and how long it will take, or if it is in fact possible to have a restaurant there and what restrictions exist."

"So, does it seem likely I could get keys by Christmas?" he asked expectantly.

"It really depends on the answers to all those questions and more. But it's possible."

"Great! What else will you help me with?" he asked.

Ben seemed very keen to keep Tamsin involved in the development of the restaurant, but her job ended at the sale.

"Not much. I will basically get out of the way after you agree on a price and a tentative date to take the keys, and just keep an eye on things until it's very close to being completed. Someone from my office will be helping with more of the details. My job is showing property and we have people who do more of the paperwork and admin around sales."

"I see," said Ben, sounding disappointed. "Can you help me with things like managing contractors, interior designers or finding things I need?"

"Those aren't really services of an estate agent, or things we provide. I'm sure you would have much better connections to top professionals than I would, if I'm honest about it."

Tamsin thought that Ben was trying to find a way to keep her involved in the process of getting the restaurant ready, but she had no idea why.

She was attracted to Ben, who had a charm about him that was more than skin deep, but given his wealth and lifestyle, she didn't think there was any way that he felt the same about her, or that if he did, he would act on it. He was surely on several most eligible bachelor lists and women must be queuing up to date and possibly even marry him.

"Since you are here, can we go to the cottage again today with Gran and see it one further time?"

"Yes, we can do that. I have the keys with me," she said, very thankful that she hadn't left them at her flat in London.

"If I'm going to buy the building, I need to spend much more time here than I have been, and Gran is right, staying at Gideon's house isn't ideal. I could stay here at the Hall, but…"

"And you think you would be able to take the cottage as soon as possible?"

"Yes, I'd love to have the keys and move in as soon as possible. Subject to Gran's approval today, of course, since she is financing everything. It's all part of my inheritance, but funds can't be released just any time I want them. It's all managed through a trust."

Tamsin wondered if Ben's grandmother would be impressed with the cottage this time. So far, she hadn't shown any real interest in it, but then, it was a tiny three bedroom cottage, not something she would want to live in herself. Purchasing Lavender Cottage would be a business transaction as far as Lady Philippa was concerned, and Tamsin thought that she would eventually agree to whatever Ben wanted. He was thirty-five years old after all and had a plan. Tamsin could understand holding funds back for a younger person, but it seemed strange that at his age he'd not be able to make decisions like buying a house.

But what do I know about how upper class people organize and spend their money? she thought.

There were obviously millions and millions of

pounds being held for Ben, in complicated trusts set up by qualified people, and it probably made sense to release them for specific reasons only, with very tight controls.

CHAPTER 27

By eleven o'clock, they had seen the building again with Ben's grandmother, and she had given her approval. Lady Philippa had agreed that it was a good space for the restaurant and instructed Tamsin to make an offer and keep her informed of the response. She made an offer at two million three hundred thousand, which she considered to be fair, since the building had tremendous intrinsic value, but was in need of a complete overhaul, no matter what purpose it was used for. As this figure was quite a bit under the asking price of two million eight hundred and fifty thousand pounds, Tamsin thought there would be a lot of negotiation to do before the seller would agree. But she smiled and looked at Ben, who was beaming with excitement.

When they arrived at Lavender Cottage, Tamsin opened the door for Ben and Lady Philippa and stayed outside to look at the garden and the pond. The lawn was completely overgrown now, and getting worse each time she came to see the cottage.

After a short time, Ben came out with his grandmother and said excitedly, "You know what? I think this place can work for me, at least for the foreseeable future. And I need to find a place here in Oxford."

"You mean, you want to make an offer on the cottage?" Tamsin asked, unable to believe how her luck was changing.

"Yes."

"That's great news, Ben! Any special requests, such as clearing the gutters?"

"No, that's not necessary. I'll hire someone local to do that myself once I get the keys, but it would be good if the owner could tidy up the garden a little now, as all the leaves are down and it's getting quite overgrown."

"I will ask the seller," said Tamsin. She knew that Mr. Crighton would not pay for that, so she would pay for a gardener or do it herself. "What price are you proposing?" she asked.

"I think one million five hundred is fair."

"Agreed. I'll call the seller. I should just tell you now though that he has had five offers on the cottage already – including one at the asking price – and he's turned them all down."

Ben looked concerned.

"Why was that?" he asked.

"I honestly don't know. He is a friend of my boss, the owner of Red Brick Realty, so I'm going to call him first and ask him how best to position your offer in order to have the best chance that Mr. Crighton will agree to sell it to you."

Tamsin locked the cottage door and walked to the Bentley, which Ben was driving. She'd never been close to a luxury car like this before, and when she got in and sat down, she thought how beautiful it was. The leather seats were as soft as butter, and even the stitching on the seats was as exquisite as the rest of the car. It was extremely opulent, thought Tamsin.

The morning had turned out to be a pleasant surprise, with two offers to be made. All the trips to Oxford were finally paying off, Tamsin thought. In the space of two weeks, she had sold four properties, although it had taken twelve months of very hard work to get here.

Now that things were going in the right direction, she could focus on getting her independence back by finding a new place to live and sorting out her plans for university.

CHAPTER 28

"Tamsin, shall we get some lunch?" Ben asked once he started the car.

"Sounds good. Plenty of time before my train," said Tamsin.

"Gran, I'll take you home, shall I?"

"Yes, thank you. Excellent work, Tamsin. I'm happy that we have found a place for Harry to live, and that he can now focus on getting things ready for an April opening."

"Thank you, Lady Philippa. I'm glad to help. If they accept your offers, the process of conveyancing can start immediately on both the building and the cottage."

"Wonderful," said Lady Philippa as they pulled up at Tansley Hall and she got out of the car.

Ben and Tamsin drove on, choosing a vegan restaurant for lunch, just on the edge of the town centre. It wasn't fancy, but it had good ratings, so they decided to give it a try. Given the lunch crowd was just dispersing, they had plenty of room and it was quiet.

"I have a charity event next Friday evening, and I wonder if you'd like to join me, Tamsin."

Tamsin thought for a moment. The invitation had come out of the blue, and Ben had asked her immediately after they were seated, as if he'd been planning to ask but hadn't found the right time. Seeming as though he had expected her to hesitate, he quickly continued, "My father is the Chairman of the Board, and I go every year. It's a black tie event, and is being held at the Queen's House, Greenwich."

"Well, that sounds really lovely, Ben.

Tamsin wondered why Ben was asking her to a charity event. Soon their business together would be done.

"But, I don't have anything suitable to wear to an event like that."

"That's not a problem. We can get you something from the Hall, or, if you would permit me, I would be happy to pay for a gown, of your choosing."

A gown? For a ball?

The evening sounded like it would be a society event, if that was the term for it, at which she'd be scrutinized by every other woman there. Her anxiety would be hard to control and her nerves likely to let her down. She might say the wrong thing, or worse, back out at the last moment, frozen with fear.

Could she handle it?

Even if she kept her nerves in check, a ball gown would be very expensive, and wasn't something she could afford to buy. She also didn't want to be indebted to Ben for anything, or to any man, from now on.

How and where she would find something in a week that would be suitable, she did not know.

Maybe she could just borrow the dress she'd worn the other night.

She needed time to think and process this information, but Ben kept talking and she tried to listen.

"I'm coming down to London on Monday. We could

meet in Marylebone, and go to two or three boutiques to see what they have, if you are up for that."

"What is the charity, Ben?" Tamsin asked, trying to stall for time to come up with a reasonable excuse for why she could not go with him.

"It's a private wildlife foundation, which my Godfather started in the nineteen seventies."

A family charity, as well.

More pressure.

She started to worry.

Besides not having anything to wear, what bothered Tamsin was that this was definitely going to be a DATE. And at the moment, she didn't have time for men. She had plans, and she needed to focus on achieving them.

But on the other hand, what harm could it do to accompany Ben to something that obviously mattered greatly to him? She'd been out with him three times already, if you counted dinner at the Hall, and was doing so now. Those hadn't been dates, so attending an event as his plus one needn't be considered one either.

"Ok, but let's agree that if we can't find anything on Monday, you will just bring down the dress and shoes I wore for dinner last night, and I'll wear those, ok?"

"Agreed," he said, as their food arrived.

CHAPTER 29

As she got out of the Bentley at Oxford Station, on her way to catch the train back to London, Tamsin still hadn't heard back from either seller who she had called as soon as they left the cottage. She told Ben she'd be in touch the minute she had any news on the offers he and Lady Philippa had made, and said goodbye.

When she settled into her seat on the train, she went over the last twenty-four hours again in her head. It had been a whirlwind. She didn't really understand why Ben would bother buying a building, setting up and running a restaurant, when he didn't have to work at all. Maybe it was the fact that we all need purpose in our lives, she thought, and being rich just wasn't enough. She considered that maybe after time, having a lot of money would wear off, and you'd have to make yourself useful in the world. And if you were born with wealth, like Ben, you'd need to find things to do in life.

If both sellers agreed to the offers from Lady Philippa, Tamsin would be paid quite a large commission. That coupled with what she would get from the sale of the flats would make a very big change to her life.

It wouldn't be enough to have a deposit to buy her own flat, but it was certainly enough for a rental deposit, to take a little vacation and to pay the first instalment at City University for January. She couldn't believe how things were all falling into place. The university fees were due very soon and she thought she'd better check when, so she didn't miss the deadline.

She really wanted a break, and considered where she'd like to take a vacation. What would be warm in December, and on the ocean, but not somewhere everyone else she knew had been?

Malibu. Catalina Island. Santa Barbara. Those places all sounded very exciting, as did Carmel. She starting searching Carmel on her phone and then checked the date the university fees were due, which she had forgotten to do each time she remembered.

Up popped an ad from the University of Texas Law School, calling for foreign students to apply for the January intake and full scholarships. All applications were due November thirtieth, just two weeks away.

Tamsin dived into the details about the university on their website, and, never having been to Texas, looked at a map of the city of Austin to see whether it was near any water. It was on a river. So, not the ocean, but no different really than living in London, on the Thames. Since she had grown up on the ocean, she felt a strong pull to always live by water, which is why Hammersmith suited her so well.

The fees there were the same per semester as they were in London, but in US Dollars, which meant it was less expensive for Tamsin than the local London fees. The university had a good rating and it looked like a nice campus.

Could this be the answer to my problems? Tamsin wondered.

Only if it was a full scholarship. She looked at what was required for the application process, and it didn't seem to be too onerous. She could probably pull it together on time if she made the effort. Tamsin knew she tended to leave things, especially important things, until just before they were due, and then kicked herself for doing so. If she wanted to make this deadline, she would need to start working on her application this weekend.

But did she want to go to university in the States? The most important thing to Tamsin was qualifying as a barrister, and where she did that didn't matter at this point. Anything that would make it more affordable would help, and here was a university looking for overseas students, for whom there were scholarships available, including a fully paid place to stay on campus.

She'd never get the scholarship of course, knowing her grades were not top of her class, but why not try? She bookmarked the site and went back to look at places to visit in California for the rest of the journey to London.

❅ ❅ ❅

Carmel sounded divine. Beach, sun, and even though it would be December, it would still be warmer than London. All of the ads made it look like a place geared towards couples, but she didn't care. There were many excellent shops and restaurants, and she needed a break.

But maybe she was getting ahead of herself. She still had to ask Becca for a short term loan for the rental deposit, until she got paid for the Shoreditch flat sales. *One thing at a time,* she thought. The priority now was getting the application for the University of Texas filled in.

She resolved to get going on the application later that evening and to call Nico to enlist his help in hunting for a flat. Andrew would help her, but he was in Milan and wouldn't be back for week. Nico and Tamsin had worked together at the university bookstore at Bristol, and had been friends ever since. He was single, lived in Stoke Newington and said he'd be happy to help her figure out where to live and see places when she'd texted to ask him for help.

At the moment, she didn't know where she wanted to live, so to narrow that down she needed some input from Nico, and then Becca, since they knew her best.

CHAPTER 30

Monday 18th November

By Monday morning, Tamsin was already tired of trying to find a flat. She'd been searching all weekend online, and could not narrow down the locations. Although she had a decent budget now, she just wasn't sure where she wanted to live. She'd been messaging Nico since Saturday, and he had suggested Islington, which she had already thought of, and Becca hadn't any ideas. She lived in Dulwich in a detached home and had two kids, so schools were her priority. She told Tamsin that her idea of where best to live as a single woman was out of date, since she had been married ten years. Someone at work had suggested Bow Church or Devons Road, but both were a long way from work and required multiple trains to get there.

Canary Wharf had lots of new developments, she knew. Maybe something over there would be good. She could take the Jubilee or DLR directly from Canary Wharf Station, and be at work in a reasonable time. Since Red Brick Realty didn't have any other branches, or any flats for rent in the east end, she registered with other estate agencies in Canary Wharf, Angel and Stoke Newington, all places she liked to spend time.

At eleven-thirty, she had a call from Mr. Crighton, and to her surprise, he agreed to sell the cottage for two hundred thousand pounds less than the asking price. Maybe James had spoken to him, and told him that it was overpriced to begin with and had been on the market a year now, so buyers were wondering what was wrong with it. The listing had become stale and the house really needed some upkeep to the outdoors if he wanted to keep it on the market and show it through the winter. Whatever James had said, if he had said anything, worked. She was just about to call Ben and Lady Philippa when the phone rang.

"Tamsin Davies, Red Brick Realty."

"Tamsin. Hello. This is George Grant, from Minneapolis. I'm the owner of the building for sale on the river in Oxford. My realtor is not answering this morning, so I thought I'd call you directly. I received your offer yesterday by email and thank you for it, but the price is just not where it needs to be. I wasn't going to respond at all, thinking your buyer is not serious, offering five hundred thousand pounds less than my asking price, but I wanted to give you a courtesy call. I assume my agent has already contacted you to tell you this?"

"No, he hasn't."

"I'm sure you know the building is worth much more than what has been offered. Please let your buyer know they will need to bring the price up substantially if they want me to take their offer seriously."

"I will do. Thank you for calling, Mr. Grant."

At that, she knew she'd better call Ben, and Lady Philippa, to give them both the good news, and the bad news.

But first, she needed some air. She stepped out onto Kings Road, and it was full of people, as it always was. The energy was high and she remembered she had to meet Ben later that afternoon in Marylebone to try on dresses for Friday night.

She had forgotten all about that this morning and had put on jeans and an oversized off the shoulder jumper, knowing she wasn't seeing clients. It was one of her favourites, from All Saints. They had the best clothes for hanging out and casual wear, but how this look would go down in high end boutiques, she didn't know. She would never step into a boutique in Marylebone selling evening gowns on her own, since she couldn't afford to buy anything, but she figured that with Ben there, they wouldn't be quite so judgmental of her outfit. She grabbed a sandwich at Chez Paris, not having to queue since it was early for the lunch crowd, and headed back to the office.

CHAPTER 31

Tamsin wondered if she should call Ben now, or wait to talk to him when she saw him later. He'd be leaving soon to drive back to London, so if she wanted to talk to him, she should call him before he left. But as her client was actually Lady Philippa, she wasn't sure who to call. She texted Ben to say she had news and asked if he was with Lady Philippa, because she had an update for her.

Ben replied saying that as it happened, he was at the Hall and so was his grandmother, and asked if she could call right away. Tamsin called Ben on WhatsApp and he picked up, with video. She turned her camera on as well, while he got his grandmother to come to the phone.

Tamsin told them both about the accepted offer on Lavender Cottage, and the request for a higher price on the building on the water. Lady Philippa said she was delighted about the cottage and would consider the seller's feedback on the building and think about a new price to offer.

When she dropped off the call, Ben asked, "All ready for later? Dress shopping?"

He sounded excited about it, so Tamsin hoped he wasn't getting ahead of himself, expecting her to look like a princess, transformed by a frock that cost a fortune.

"Oh yes, ready to meet you at Civello, at four o'clock. We're only going to two stores and then calling it quits, right?"

Tamsin now realized she hadn't put her Spanx on, and would likely be bulging out of whatever dresses she tried on, not having shapewear to hold herself in. As a size ten and sometimes twelve, this wasn't a problem for Tamsin normally, since she didn't wear form fitting or tight clothes very often. But she thought that something to smooth things out under an elegant dress was a good idea.

She had it in her mind to get a black dress, very simple and plain, and the cheapest one they had as well. She hoped it would not be a mistake allowing Ben to buy her a dress, or going with him to an event that was important to his family. He'd texted her the invitation and it had also arrived by hand delivery at the office earlier this morning. It was very formal and printed on thick white paper in gold letters, and gold leaf flakes, not likely real, Tamsin thought, fell out of the envelope when she pulled the card out.

The official name of the event was the Oakwood Autumnal Ball, to be precise. She had Googled the charity and saw that it hit the news headlines every year. She hadn't realized how famous Ben's father Charles, the Eighth Earl of Tansley, was. Most of the pictures she saw from last year's event had Pepper in the centre of each frame, in a gorgeous outfit, dripping in jewels, with Ben's dad to the side. Pepper was a stunning woman and at forty-six was quite a bit younger than her husband. Her long wavy ginger hair made her stand out in every crowd. Charles Smythe-Jones was a handsome sixty-three-year-old, with greying temples and a slim build. He was tall as well, over six foot, and cut a very suave figure in black tie formal wear.

Now she started to panic, thinking that Pepper would be there, along with many other aristocratic women, and she feared they would all judge her. But Pepper had a broken arm, so would she attend an event like this with an injury like that? Tamsin wondered. Probably not.

She'd have to ask Ben whether Pepper intended to come to the ball. If so, it would be important not to buy the same colour dress as her. That would not be classy, she thought, showing up wearing the same colour dress as her date's step-mother. That rule applied even at weddings, never mind balls. Did they still have protocols about commoners not wearing certain colours when there were members of the aristocracy present? Or could that just be made up nonsense she read in a trashy book? She texted Ben to ask what colour Pepper would be wearing, and if she was attending. He replied Black, and yes, she would be there.

❄ ❄ ❄

In a panic, Tamsin called Becca.

"What's wrong, Tamsin?" Becca asked.

"Becs, I am just not sure about this. Ben has asked me to go with him this Friday to a charity ball, of which his father is Chairman of the Board, and he's buying me a dress today so I can go."

"Okay, and what is wrong with that?"

"Well, you know. This is a ball. There is going to be press. His dad is an earl. But all that aside, the dress is going to cost hundreds, if not thousands of pounds, based on where we are shopping for it, and I'm not sure that this is a good idea. I'm just about over Jason, and here I am, putting another man in his place and taking fancy gifts from him. Does this sound normal to you?"

"It's been two years since you and Jason broke up, Tamsin, and I know that his recent idiotic behaviour threw you for a loop, but it's time to get out there again. Start dating, and having fun. Have sex. That will take your mind off Jason.

"So what if a future Earl wants to buy you a dress and take you to a ball? Sounds like great fun. Just enjoy it. You are not making a commitment to him, and he must know that."

Tamsin was silent.

"Are you still there?" asked Becca. "Tamsin?" she tried again.

"I don't know..." said Tamsin, wondering how to get out of going to the ball.

"I'll try on some dresses. But I think I had better tell Ben that I am NOT looking for a relationship right now. I have to go to go back to uni and get my law qualifications. I need to get my own flat. Getting involved with anyone right now is just too much."

"You can tell him that," said Becca. "Just keep things light, and he will follow that lead, I'm sure. For all you know, he just doesn't have a date for some reason this time, and he's asking you because the two of you get on and he obviously thinks it would be fun to have you there with him. Trust me, it will be ok. Just have your phone, purse and keys with you, so you can get home when you want, and not have to rely on him. And call me if you need to."

"Ok, thanks, Becca. I will pull myself together, since it's already three-thirty and I need to get over to Marylebone."

Tamsin hung up and went to splash her face with water. She hadn't even put make-up on today, just moisturizer. Maybe that was a good thing. She didn't want to get anything on the dresses she would try on, so being without make-up was understandable, wasn't it? She put on some lip balm, combed her hair, and headed off to the tube.

CHAPTER 32

As soon as the train left the station, Tamsin felt sick, as she often did travelling on the Tube. Something about being underground and in a low ceilinged carriage made her feel unwell. It was loud, noisy and dirty. But today her uneasiness was worse than usual, as she was nervous all of a sudden about seeing Ben.

Keep *cool*, she told herself.

It's just *dress* shopping.

When she got out at Bond Street Station, she had to check the map on her phone to find the boutique. She knew the general direction but not the actual street. The location was obvious once she found it, but hard to find while walking around on the streets of Marylebone for some reason. She never knew East from West or North from South. At least in Margate the sea was always an indicator of direction. In London, she could never figure that out.

When she was a few doors away from Civello, she texted Ben to find out where he was, not wanting to walk into the boutique by herself. He texted to say he was right behind her. She turned around and saw him, smiled, waved, and waited for him to catch up.

"Hi, Tamsin," he said, with a wide smile. She could barely resist him now that she looked at him properly, fully.

"Hi, Ben. This place looks very expensive," she said, looking at the front of the boutique and furrowing her brow in disapproval.

"It's fine, don't worry about that. We need to make sure that you have a knockout dress and this is one of the best boutiques for gowns in the city, according to Pepper, who has an account here."

"Did you ask her where to buy a dress?"

Tamsin was horrified, thinking that Ben had involved Pepper in this and now worried that Pepper would think she was using Ben, forcing him to buy her a dress and take her to an important ball, although neither could be farther from the truth. *He* had asked *her* to the event and had kindly offered to get her something suitable to wear.

What average woman would have the right dress for a fancy dress ball in her closet?

No one Tamsin knew had any dresses suitable for charity balls, that was for sure.

"No. I told my father I had invited you and he suggested Civello and one other place where Pepper buys all her gowns or has them made."

"Ok. Let's do this," she said as she took a deep breath, exhaled and pushed the door open to one of the most exclusive boutiques in town.

CHAPTER 33

"Good afternoon, sir," said the man who greeted them.

"Viscount Tansley," said Ben.

Tamsin nodded to the man, who straightened up his back on hearing the word Viscount.

"My Lord," said the man.

"We are here to buy a gown for Ms. Davies, who will be accompanying me to the Oakwood Autumnal Ball Friday evening at the Queen's House."

"Very well, and welcome to Civello. What colour and style do you have in mind, Madam?"

He had addressed Tamsin, but she had no idea how to reply, not knowing what would and would not be appropriate for the event. Ben spoke as she tried to think of what to say.

"Why don't you bring three dresses, not black, and three pairs of shoes for Ms. Davies to try on? Thank you," he said.

"Certainly, my Lord." And with that, he left them.

The attendant walked by different dresses hanging on racks, and eventually selected a strapless green silk gown, with a large crinoline and hundreds of crystals on the skirt, a fitted navy blue velvet embroidered gown, with one shoulder strap, and a turquoise gown with a plunging neckline and removable crinoline, open at the front, with a short skirt, which was designed to show off legs from the knee down. Tamsin thought that one was the most beautiful, but possibly a bit too revealing. The boutique assistant helping them, Felipe, also brought three pairs of crystal encrusted matching shoes, in silver, black and blue, for Tamsin to try on.

A female seamstress joined her in the dressing room to help do up each gown and ensure they fit properly, pinning them where necessary, before Tamsin stepped out of the change room. Thankfully, she also brought in the right undergarments as well.

Each dress was more luxurious than the last, from the colours, to the fabric, to the embellishments, be it crystals or beads or embroidery, and she started by trying on the green silk gown. It was stunning and fit Tamsin very well. It was paired with the silver high heeled shoes, with crystals, matching the dress. The attendant also brought long green gloves, as it was sleeveless, and they elevated the elegance of the dress.

She looked at Ben for an opinion when she stepped out of the room, and he said of the green dress, "It's really lovely, but perhaps too flashy for an environment focussed event like this one. Even though green is a great colour on you."

When she tried on the blue dress, she felt very grown up, sexy and in control. This would be the one, she thought. It was navy blue velvet, with embroidered flowers in black and silver thread on the skirt and bodice. The same shoes in black this time made for the most elegant look. There were two versions of this dress, one with a crinoline and one without. The more fitted version hugged her hips and breasts and made her look stunning.

Ben was speechless when she stepped out of the changing room in the form fitting version.

"Yes," he said. "That's the dress."

She twirled around and looked at herself in all the mirrors, which gave a full body view from every angle. She almost didn't recognize herself, she looked so good. Ben looked at her for a view on what she thought, and she smiled and nodded in agreement, that this was the one.

She tried on the turquoise gown and although it didn't seem possible, she looked even better in this dress. The plunging neckline and way the fabric laid across her chest created the most stunning figure she had ever cut and the dress was like a dream. But the elegance of the fabric and design would likely outshine other women. She could tell that, and it seemed Ben agreed. He said only "Wow," when she came out of the dressing room.

"Beautiful, but perhaps not for this?" she suggested.

"Yes, I would like to spend an evening with you wearing that dress, alone on our own, not in a room with hundreds of other people."

The sum total of the dress, shoes and matching clutch, which she chose in black silk, came to twelve thousand, six hundred pounds and twenty-five pence. That was several times more money than Tamsin had ever had in the bank at one time. Accepting this as a gift was insane, and she knew it. But she was going to have the time of her life at the ball.

"Do you have a hairstylist who can do your hair in advance, Tamsin?" Ben asked when they left the boutique.

She shook her head no, she did not.

"I mean, I have someone who cuts my hair, of course. But I don't think he'd be able to do my hair for an event like this," she said.

"I will send a driver for you, but it will be a slow drive from Hammersmith to Greenwich, so we would be better off going directly from my place in Kensington, which is closer to the venue. I could organize stylists to come to my house who can do your hair and also your make-up, if you would like. My stylist will be there anyway, doing a last trim for me, and Gary, my footman, will be bringing my clothing and boutonnière. We could get ready together if you like."

Tamsin hadn't really considered hair and make-up, but of course how they were done was essential.

"That sounds great, Ben."

"I'll ask Helen to come as well, and to bring the right jewels."

It was just after six and Tamsin didn't know what to do with the bags when they left the boutique, as she'd have to take the Tube. Carrying the dress and shoes on a crowded rush hour train would be awkward and difficult for anyone, but especially for Tamsin, who hated taking the Tube. The items were already impossible to hold onto, being in large bags and boxes.

"Here," said Ben, taking them off her hands. "Let's put these in the car and I'll take them to my house," said Ben as they approached his vehicle. "In fact, I'm having dinner tonight with some friends. Would you like to join us?"

Tamsin worried that her very casual outfit was not fit for purpose but was happy to be invited and wanted to have dinner with Ben and meet his friends.

"Um, well," she said, tugging at her sleeve, "This is all I have to wear. Would this be ok for where we are going?"

"Ha, yes! We are just dining at my place."

"Ok then, sounds good."

"Great, hop in. Giles is cooking tonight, and he will be arriving soon. I'll give him a ring now and make sure he knows to bring enough food for one more guest."

Tamsin got in the passenger side of the car and they started driving to Ben's six storey townhouse in Kensington. When they arrived, Tamsin was surprised by what she saw, but kept it to herself. The townhouse had an electronic gate that prevented anyone entering the property, including cars that wanted to pull in, and the neighbour's house on the right hand side had two very large men, who Tamsin thought were security guards, standing out front of their gate.

She supposed that in Holland Park, Kensington, private security might be needed, but it made her feel less safe, since she wondered what they were protecting. Maybe the neighbours were famous, or they just had a lot of valuables in their house.

Ben drove the car up to the garage and the electronic gate locked behind them. All the outdoor lights came on as he drove in, since it was now dark outside. Tamsin thought they must be motion sensors and they came on again when she stepped out of the car.

The house was all white, with large columns out front, and the most beautiful house that Tamsin had ever seen, next to Tansley Hall. Almost as soon as they had opened the front door to the house, someone buzzed from the road.

"Giles is here," Ben said after checking the camera, and opened the gate to let him in.

Giles opened the front door and shouted, "It's me! I need a hand!"

Ben hurried to the front door from the living room, where they had just sat down with drinks, and Tamsin followed.

"Giles! Great to see you! This is Tamsin."

"Hi, Tamsin," Giles said as he reached out a hand, while placing numerous bags on the floor. "I've heard a lot about you these past couple of weeks. Ben is very impressed with your ability to negotiate real estate deals."

She would accept that compliment, but hoped that Ben was taken with more about her than just her real estate skills.

"Nice to meet you, Giles. And thank you for having me join your dinner tonight. Ben just invited me earlier today, so I hope I'm not putting you out."

"Not at all. I hope you like French food."

"Absolutely."

They all went into the kitchen and Giles unpacked the food he had brought, most of which he had prepared in his own kitchen and was almost ready.

"Wine?" Ben asked them both.

"Yes, please," Tamsin and Giles both said at once.

"Red for me, and white for you two," said Ben as he poured their wine.

"Cheers," they all said and clinked glasses.

"So, what's for dinner?" asked Ben.

"Chicken cordon bleu, a new grapefruit salad I have

just invented and baked raspberry tarts with lemon sorbet for dessert."

"Sounds delicious," said Tamsin. "Who else is coming this evening, Ben?" she asked.

"Just Suzie and Patrick. Friends from Oxford."

"So Tamsin, Ben tells me you are going to be his date this year for the Oakwood Autumnal on Friday night. Are you sure you are up for that?"

Tamsin was a bit confused by the question and looked at Ben. She hadn't had time to let it sink in yet, that she was going to a ball. Was there something to worry about?

"Don't scare her off Giles," Ben said, only half-joking.

"No. Sorry, Tamsin," said Giles, laughing. "What I meant was, it's a big deal with the press and everything."

"Oh, I wasn't aware of that."

"You will be fine. I will handle them, not to worry," said Ben. "The last thing I want is another woman being put off by the press that sometimes follows me around, although they haven't been doing so lately. It's stressful for me to have cameras and flashing lights in my face, never mind someone who has never experienced unwanted attention from the media."

The doorbell rang and Suzie and Patrick greeted Ben with hugs, and more food. They brought a gorgeous bouquet of flowers, wine, port, which they had just bought on a trip to Portugal, and some fresh vegetables, which looked like they came straight from a farm. As they entered the kitchen, they both said, "Hi, Tamsin."

"Hi!" she replied.

Suzie went to wash the lettuce she had brought, and Tamsin asked Ben if there was anything she could do to help. He said no and that she should just relax and get ready to enjoy Giles's great food.

"So, Tamsin," Patrick said, "Ben tells us you have found him the perfect spot for the new restaurant. We can't wait to see it. Which building is it?"

Remembering they were from Oxford, she said, "The one next to the florist."

"Oh, right. That is a lovely building," said Suzie. "I remember thinking that just recently when I walked by. It's going to make an excellent venue for Giles and Ben's new venture."

They sat down and had more wine, while Giles continued cooking.

Suzie asked "And what are you wearing to the ball, Tamsin?"

She explained what the dress looked like, and asked if Suzie would be there.

"Oh yes, we'll be there. Patrick's father Justin and Ben's dad Charles are good friends. We go every year."

Finally, dinner was served. Giles said that he wanted honest feedback on the meal, as he was considering making it one of the features of the new restaurant's spring menu.

"Very good, Giles," Patrick said.

"Excellent, Giles. The chicken is really tender and delicious," said Suzie.

"Tamsin, what do you think?" Giles asked.

"It's really good. I can taste the rosemary, but just a hint, and the lemon as well. And with the mashed potatoes, it's a fabulous main. Just the sort of comforting food you need in winter."

"What about the salad? Do you like it?"

She did. It was beautiful to look at, with the pink grapefruit, crunchy thanks to the walnuts, and a little sweet from the honey and mint.

"Superb," said Ben. "You have nailed it again, Giles."

Tamsin wasn't sure if she should stay, once the others started to leave, but Ben asked her to stay back and have a nightcap before going, so she agreed.

"Well, that was lovely, Ben. Thank you for inviting me, and for everything else today. The dress really is an extravagance, so I appreciate it. I hope I will be able to use it again sometime."

"I am certain you will," he said. "We have a Christmas party at the Hall in December, and it would wonderful if you could come to that as well, Tamsin. Although you would not need a gown, since it's much more casual."

She wasn't sure what was going on here. Since this afternoon, Ben had started behaving more as if they were a couple than in a professional relationship. She didn't mind, but she wasn't sure what the cues were telling her. It had been a long time since she'd had feelings for anyone other than Jason, but she couldn't deny it much longer – she had them for Ben. Trying not to overthink, she poured some more wine and just relaxed.

Ben was sitting in one corner of the couch, and he held out his hand, which she took. He pulled her in close and she leaned back on his shoulder. He was very warm and smelled amazing. Perhaps she'd had a little too much to drink, but she was feeling very comfortable in his arms. He kissed her head and said,

"Thank you for coming over, Tamsin. You looked absolutely stunning today in the dress, in all the dresses actually, and I am so happy you agreed to come for dinner and meet my friends."

At this she sat up and asked him, "What are we doing here, Ben? Are we starting to date?"

"I don't know. I hope so. Would you like us to?"

"I would," she said, surprised at her answer, since she hadn't thought about it until they were shopping for the dress earlier. "But I am not looking for a relationship right now, Ben. I need to be honest about that. You are charming, funny and kind, and of course, drop dead gorgeous, but my life is a bit messy right now."

She meant to go on, but he pulled her back towards him and they began to kiss. His lips were soft and he was now kissing her neck, and her shoulder, and she could not help herself but give in. She kissed him back and they got up and walked to the bedroom.

In the middle of the night she woke up, and once her eyes had adjusted to the dark, she could make out Ben's silhouette in the bed next to her. He was very sexy, and muscular. They had taken their time making love, getting to know each other's bodies, as only new lovers can. Her body ached for him right now, but she didn't want to wake him. She put her hand on his ribbed abs, laid her head on his chest and started to fall back asleep. He turned towards her, they both opened their eyes and he kissed her softly, pulling her closer to him.

CHAPTER 34

In the morning, she woke up to the smell of bacon and freshly brewed coffee.

"Morning, beautiful," Ben said as he came into the bedroom and leaned down to kiss her on the lips. "I hope you like bacon. Suzie and Patrick brought it from their farm in Oxford. It's smoked streaky and really good."

"Morning, handsome," she said. "Yes, you will not find a woman who loves bacon more than me."

"Well then, come down to the kitchen when you are ready and have some breakfast. I've also made eggs with a tomato feta salad and sourdough toast. It's all waiting for you."

Tamsin got up, looked at herself in the mirror and splashed her face with water, before joining Ben in the kitchen. She had slept better than she had for many months. And the sex, that now seemed like a dream. She was impressed she could remember how it was done, it had been so long, and with how attentive Ben had been. She could get used to this. But now she had to get to work, and home first to change, but what a night it had been!

Since she and Jason had broken up over two years ago, she hadn't slept with anyone. Not a single night of sex for over two years, until last night. And it was all just so natural. Not planned, not analysed, just normal and frankly, incredible.

Who knew Ben had that much passion? He was such a gentle, sweet guy, but passionate and attentive to her needs. So unlike Jason. She had been repressing her sexual desires for so long, and hadn't really met anyone she wanted to spend the night with, until now. It had certainly been worth waiting for.

After breakfast she said, "I really have to get going now, Ben. I need to get home, change and then to the office. I have so much to do before Christmas, and it's just getting busier each day."

"Of course. Let me drive you home."

"Thanks, Ben, that will save me a lot of time."

She hadn't told him anything about Jason yet. That could wait. Jason was the past, but he was still part of her life, and would be, until she got out of the flat. When Ben dropped her off, she said, "I'd invite you in, but I need to hurry. We have a daily meeting at ten o'clock that we all need to be at, so I have to rush."

"Raincheck then," he said, smiling.

"Absolutely. I'll call you later. Please find out what Lady Philippa wants to counter back with as a new price to the seller, given he rejected her first offer."

"Will do. Bye, Tamsin," he said, blowing her a kiss.

She blew him one back and went inside to change.

CHAPTER 35

Tamsin was so excited, she had to call Becca.

"Becs," she said as she pulled her jeans on.

"Tamsin, what's wrong?" Becca was worried as it was only seven-thirty in the morning, a strange time for Tamsin to call.

"Nothing. It's all good news. I have sold the Shoreditch flats, and the cottage in Oxford, and I slept with Ben last night."

"You WHAT?!"

"Yes. I did."

"Oh, my goodness," she said. "And? How was it?"

"Let's just say I have not had a night of passion like that in a very long time."

"Good for you, Tamsin. I'm proud of you for getting out there again."

"There is something else. I need your help with a rental deposit, just to tide me over for the next four weeks until I get paid for the sale of the flats."

"Of course. How much do you need?"

"No idea. I haven't even figured out where I'm going to live. But I'll let you know soon. I have to get going to work."

"Ok T, call me later."

"Will do. Bye."

"Bye."

Tamsin rushed out of the house and to the office, making it just in time for the ten o'clock daily meeting.

Sammy needed to talk to her when it was over, as he was having trouble with Antony V.

"What's the issue, Sammy?"

"Antony's solicitor has not called the sellers of the second flat yet. Could he be changing his mind?"

"I don't know. Let's hope not. Drop him an email, copy me and the solicitors, and then call him in an hour or two to make sure that sale starts moving. We are running out of time, Sammy, so that has to be sorted out today."

Tamsin made a list of the other things she had to do, which was long. First, she needed to know what Lady Philippa was willing to pay for the building. Even if they did agree terms in the next day or so, it was not likely Ben could get the keys until January and that would really affect his timeline for opening the restaurant. But there was little she could do at this point, until an offer was agreed and the lawyers started to get involved.

As for the other sale, after having confirmed a new price, she needed to ensure Mr. Crighton was instructing his solicitor on the sale of Lavender Cottage. Ben would have given his legal team a heads up by now that he and his gran had made a successful offer on the cottage, but just to be sure, she'd check with him later that he hadn't forgotten to do that.

Finally, she would have to get Sammy to follow up with Antony V by the end of the day to make sure he was doing everything he could to get the flats sold on time.

Her advance on the commission of those sales depended on it, and she was planning to borrow money from Becca only until that came in.

Right now, Tamsin felt like she was building a house of cards, with all the due dates and dependencies on things that were not in her control.

And there was the personal to do list on top of all this, which included deciding where to live, and filling in the University of Texas application, which she had mostly finished on the weekend. She hadn't told anyone about that idea yet. It could wait. She wasn't likely to get accepted, but it was worth trying. Why worry her parents with something that might never happen?

The only thing on the list that she was really looking forward to was booking a little escape to Carmel for the week between Christmas and New Year. And the ball. Of course she was looking forward to the ball.

By two o'clock, Tamsin had a new price from Lady Philippa that she was willing to pay for the building in Oxford, and the issues with Antony V had sorted themselves out, so the flat sales were progressing.

The building on the river was listed for two million, eight hundred and fifty thousand pounds, and in checking with James, he said that was about right, if not a bit low. Lady Philippa now wanted Tamsin to make an offer at two million six hundred thousand pounds. That was three hundred thousand pounds more than her original offer. She hoped it would be enough.

Tamsin had tried to reach the estate agent for the building a few times, but had no reply, and since the seller had called her directly, she now tried him, but wasn't able to get through. He was in the US, so they only had about four hours of each working day to reach each other. Hopefully she could sort this out today.

CHAPTER 36

Not having reached the seller, Tamsin went home and after dinner, she started to think seriously about where she really wanted to live. North London? East London? What was close to both work and university and in her budget? It was most likely she was going to be taking classes part time at night and in that case, she would want to live close to campus, if she could afford it.

Looking online, she couldn't find anything suitable for two thousand pounds a month in Angel. And that was the highest she could pay per month. Ideally, she would find something a lot less expensive than that for a one bedroom flat in a decent neighbourhood.

Stoke Newington options were marginally better, but there was still nothing good at the moment. She turned to Canary Wharf, and there she found she could get a one bedroom flat, with a balcony, within her budget. She lined up a few to see on Friday morning and planned to take the day off.

She called Nico, to see if he could go with her to look at flats. He was going to Barcelona on Saturday but agreed to join her for viewings she wanted to do on Friday morning. Since Nico worked shifts as the manager of a high end private club, he often had time during the day to do things, like helping a mate find a new flat. Nico had lived in Canary Wharf for a few years, so he knew which buildings were the best.

Between them they whittled the various options down to three. They would see one flat in Millharbour, one in Poplar and one in Island Gardens, which wasn't really Canary Wharf, but close. Each flat had one bedroom, and the one in Millharbour had a balcony and a parking space, even though Tamsin didn't need it. Things were looking up, Tamsin felt.

Ben called and asked if Tamsin would like to go with him to Suzie and Patrick's for dinner the following Saturday. Suzie had asked him if he and Tamsin would like to visit them in Oxford for a meal before dinner had been served last night, and Ben had told her that he and Tamsin were just friends, to which Suzie had replied, "Yeah, right, Ben."

After spending the night together, Ben knew that he and Tamsin could not deny that there was something happening between them, so he asked Tamsin if she would like to come with him.

"Um," said Tamsin, biting her lower lip. She worried things might be moving too quickly with Ben, and she hesitated to reply.

Sensing something was holding her back, Ben said, "They have a lovely farm in Oxfordshire, and I think they want to show it off to you, after you complimented them on their vegetables last night."

"That sounds lovely, Ben." She felt silly for holding back. "Their carrots tasted amazing, although that might have had more to do with Giles's cooking than the growing method."

"Probably both," Ben laughed. "I'll let them know we'll get there around two o'clock. Is that ok for you? I need to see the farm in daylight because Patrick wants to show me a field he is having trouble growing a crop in."

"Sure thing," said Tamsin, ready to hang up.

"Oh, Ben," she said, almost forgetting about the building purchase. "Your grandmother has asked me to revise her offer to a higher figure, but I was unable to reach the seller today or his agent, as it happens."

"Thanks for letting me know and doing your best on this. I will tell her."

"You are most welcome. I need to go and call my mum, Ben, but I'll see you Friday. I'm taking the day off to look at flats. What time should I get to your place?"

"Five o'clock, if not earlier. That will give us plenty of time for cocktails and to get ready for the evening. We will leave at six-thirty."

"Goodnight, and see you soon."

After calling her mum, Tamsin went back to look at the listings for the three flats again and felt sure there was at least one which could work. Although a lot of people did not think Canary Wharf was a great place to live, Tamsin disagreed. It had everything you could need, including grocery stores, gyms, salons, and some decent shopping.

Canary Wharf wasn't LONDON proper, since other than the converted warehouses with flats there were no old buildings or anything that would let you know you were in London, and it did look a lot like Toronto or Chicago, but Tamsin thought that maybe the shiny newness of it all meant the flats would be looked after better than in other areas of the city, and it might be a safer place to live. All the buildings on the Canary Wharf estate had security, and CCTV was everywhere, so Tamsin was getting excited about seeing the places she had booked for Friday.

So far, she'd only lived in flat shares in old houses with peeling wallpaper and damp, and in Jason's flat. His place was gorgeous, but it was time to leave. A place like this would never be in her price range, either to rent or to buy. She closed the laptop, feeling quite tired, and headed off to bed.

CHAPTER 37

Wednesday 20th November

In the morning, the estate agent for the building in Oxford called Tamsin back. They discussed the new offer amount and things were settled at the price of two million six hundred thousand pounds. The seller wanted to know how quickly Tamsin's client could complete the sale.

Knowing that Ben wanted the space as soon as possible but not wanting to sound too willing to please, she said, "My client would be happy to do what he can to take the keys by Christmas."

"Wonderful," said the agent. "That would suit the seller perfectly. Let's aim for that. I will take it off the market now, and ask him to instruct his solicitor today."

Things were going just a bit too well, thought Tamsin. In the space of four weeks, she had sold four properties, after not selling anything for almost an entire year. The commissions would be large. She would have enough money to almost pay off her remaining student debt, have enough to cover a rental deposit and rent for six months and to pay her first year of university fees.

How fortunes could be changed!

And, she was going out with a member of the

aristocracy. She didn't want to forget that minor detail. She didn't think of Ben as an 'aristocrat', but the fact he was going to be an Earl at some point did not escape her. She wondered what that would mean for her if they ever got married. But that was getting way ahead of herself. They hadn't even really been on a proper date yet. She suddenly had a thought that worried her. Was she supposed to tell James that she was in a personal relationship with a client? Did that matter? She would think about it later.

For now, she had to dash to see Becca. She'd told her that a loan of about five thousand pounds would be required, but only until she got her commission the week before Christmas. It was a lot, she knew, and she hoped it wasn't asking too much of Becs. It if was, she would say.

It would be different if it was just her money, but Becca was a married woman and Tamsin didn't know if she had even told her husband she was planning to let Tamsin borrow money. Becca had said it was no problem, so Tamsin was zipping out to buy her a small gift as a thank you; a Jo Malone perfume, which Becca liked.

When she got back to work, she told James she was planning to move house in December and just wanted to confirm that she would be paid her advance on December twentieth, as he had said. He said yes, not to worry, and she went back to work.

Tamsin called Lady Philippa to give her the good news about her offer being accepted but she didn't answer, so Tamsin left a voice mail. She then sent a text to Ben to let him know the offer had been accepted and to say that he should ask his solicitor to begin working on the purchase.

Tamsin realized that up until now, she still had no idea

what Ben was going to call his new restaurant, so she'd ask him when she saw him. She wanted to know more about him, and realized she hadn't told him anything about her own plans at this point, other than she was looking for a new flat.

She would do it soon, she thought, and headed home, pleased with herself for getting the building purchase sorted. Her plans were to order in, and do some tidying up. The flat was getting quite messy since she hadn't been home much all week.

CHAPTER 38

Friday 22nd November

At nine o'clock, Tamsin showed up at the building at Island Gardens and decided without stepping inside that the flat would not work. It seemed as though they had used photos of a completely different place, so when the estate agent arrived, a few minutes after Nico, she told him there was no point going inside, it was not the place for her. There were rubbish bins everywhere and it just didn't look like the kind of place she'd feel safe. Since she had stood her ground with Jason, she was becoming more and more assertive, and Tamsin liked this side of herself. She was embracing her ability to say no and to take charge of situations.

She and Nico went to have a coffee at a café in the shopping centre at Canary Wharf before they took the train to Poplar. It was their first chance to talk properly since meeting up earlier in the morning.

"So, Tamsin, what's new?" Nico asked.

He was always in such a great mood and had a smile that could melt a thousand hearts. Everyone loved being around Nico, and Tamsin was no exception.

"Not much, and everything, Nico."

She told him about meeting Ben and the way things were improving at work, but when she told him about the ball, he was floored.

"Do you mean *Harry* Smythe-Jones, the future Earl of Tansley?"

"Yes," Tamsin replied, perplexed at his tone, which was a mixture of curiosity and concern rolled into one.

"Why...?"

"Oh, nothing."

"Come on, Nico. What should I be worried about?"

"Caroline Martin."

"Who's 'Caroline Martin'?"

"She's Harry's ex."

"Do you know Harry?"

"He's a member of Hatchard's, of course, and until recently, we didn't have female members, but when that changed, he brought Caroline once or twice when I was working."

"And?"

"And nothing. She just, well, she has a reputation for not being very nice, that's all. For a while she was his fiancée."

"Fiancée?!"

Tamsin had to lower her voice after that, noticing that the entire café had heard her bellow out the word. Ben had not said anything about having a fiancée. In fact, he hadn't told her anything about any of his ex-girlfriends. But then, she hadn't told him anything about Jason, other than she had been in a long term relationship which had ended badly.

"So, who is this woman?"

"Lady Caroline Martin is the daughter of Lord Jessop."

"Lady Caroline?"

"Yes." said Nico, taking a bite of his mince pie. "Her mother was Antonia Martin, or Lady Jessop. Lord Jessop never remarried when his wife died, so Caroline is Lady Jessop. She uses Martin-Jessop as a surname."

"How do you know all this, Nico?"

"It's part of my job. I need to know everyone who comes to the club, how to address them, who their wives, husbands and any other partners are. It's a lot more complicated now that we have an all gender policy. We have some clients who bring multiple partners or just friends or clients, and it can be hard to know or remember the right way to address everyone. I usually wait until a guest is introduced by the member before I refer to them by any name at all, and then I need to remember what that greeting is supposed to be if I see them again."

"Sounds confusing."

"Can be, for sure. But I love my job."

Tamsin knew he did. She would never be able to remember all the different faces, never mind all the people's names.

Caroline Martin. Ben's fiancée. It would be very good to find out when that relationship had come to an end, Tamsin thought.

They headed to Millharbour after seeing a disappointing flat in Poplar. This last one seemed promising, judging by the building. It had twenty-eight floors and a gym on the ground level. There was a nice buzz about the lobby and Tamsin had a good feeling about it.

When they got inside, the flat, which was located on the twenty-second floor, opened up to an expansive view of Canary Wharf. It was stunning. The rooms were small, but it was already furnished, which was good, since Tamsin didn't have any of her own furniture. She could study in the main living and dining space at a desk that was already there.

She and Nico spent a few minutes on the balcony, and went back inside. She told the estate agent she'd have to think about it over the weekend, and get back to him early next week. He made a point about having several interested parties, which was a standard estate agent sales tactic, she knew, but in reality, even though she liked the flat, she wasn't sure it was time to make a commitment.

She wanted to see if she was accepted to the University of Texas first. It wouldn't be possible to wait for that result, as it would leave no time for her to get a flat by Christmas, but she'd hold off making a decision about where to live for another few days at least.

She thanked Nico for coming along to help her, and they hugged and parted ways at the train station. He told her to have fun at the ball and to look out for Caroline, who Nico was sure would be there.

Tamsin hurried home to pack her things and then head over to Ben's house. He'd suggested she bring some clothes for Saturday, in case she wanted to stay at his place after the ball. Things seemed to be moving quickly with Ben, and she wasn't sure that getting involved with him at any level was fair, given her own plans to go back to uni and possibly move abroad, which she hadn't told him about yet.

CHAPTER 39

Tamsin got some things together in a holdall just in case she did want to spend the night at Ben's and had called a cab, which was here now. She was ready, but she was nervous. Just a few weeks ago she could never have imagined how things would turn around for her. Back then, she was close to bankruptcy, and about to lose her flat. Now, she had money in the bank, almost, and she was dating one of the most eligible men in Britain, who she'd never heard of before she met him.

Being around all these wealthy people was causing her some anxiety. She had gotten used to it at work, just about, but the wealth and the prestige of Ben's family and his friends was on a completely different level.

Her parents were working class, like their parents, and while they didn't think being rich was anything to be ashamed about, she was feeling a wee bit inadequate at the moment, given she couldn't even afford her own shoes for the ball, which had cost twelve hundred pounds, never mind the dress and handbag Ben had bought her.

But why should any of that get in the way of having fun?

She was an intelligent, independent woman and there was nothing to worry about, she told herself. But at the same time, not having been part of this rarefied world before, she didn't want to say or do the wrong thing and worried that she might, but not know it. Before heading out, she checked the gas cooker one more time, left the sitting room light on, set the alarm and locked the door.

The cab ride to Ben's house took less time than she thought it would and she arrived at a quarter to five, which was a bit early, but Ben had said to come earlier than five o'clock if she could. Getting in was quite an experience. Tamsin had to stand on the sidewalk and press a buzzer. Someone she didn't recognize appeared on the camera and asked who she was.

"Tamsin Davies," she said. The iron gate slowly opened and she entered the driveway. The house looked intimidating now that Ben was not by her side. It was enormous and everything was perfect, inside and out. There was a lawn laid to the front, and gardens to the back. Tall topiary trees were planted in large pots on each side of the external staircase.

She was about to ring the doorbell when both front doors were opened by a man. He greeted her, said he was Gary, Ben's valet, and let her in. He showed her to a room she had not seen the other night, and found Helen waiting for her.

Another person, whose name she could not recall, but who she recognized from when she had been at Tansley Hall, asked if she would like a glass of champagne, and she giggled inwardly, thinking how Pepper would not approve.

"Yes, please," she said.

"Ma'am," said Helen, nodding to her.

"Hi, Helen," said Tamsin.

"I've brought a selection of jewellery for this evening.

There is one set that would stand out, but the choice is yours of course."

"Thank you, Helen. May I finish my drink first?"

Helen's cheeks turned red at this request for permission by Tamsin, so she re-phrased it into a statement.

"I mean, I'll finish this first, and then I'll have a look at what you have brought."

"As you wish, Ma'am."

Tamsin wasn't sure she would ever get used to the way Helen, Gary and everyone else who worked for Ben or his father demurred to them. It seemed to be right out of a historical novel. But it was real. Their jobs were to support the members of Ben's family, and their needs. They all lived full time at Tansley Hall and as far as Tamsin could tell, none of them had partners or children. But if they did, how would that work? Maybe because Ben's friends also lived like this, with full time support staff, it seemed normal to all of them. It wasn't normal for Tamsin, even if she did like being pampered.

When she finished her drink, she followed Helen to the bedroom where the gown, shoes and clutch she had selected with Ben were laid out. On the dresser were three open jewellery boxes. One held the diamond choker she had worn at the Hall. Another looked like a necklace of pink diamonds but Helen said, "Pink Sapphires, Ma'am," as if reading her mind.

In the last box was a set of jewels of the deepest and brightest red she had ever seen. There was a pair of chandelier earrings and a necklace with several red stones set in three rows, and a single large pendant hanging down. The jewellery was exquisite.

"This is a Ruby set, Ma'am. It was Lady Tansley's favourite necklace to pair with navy blue before she passed."

There was no question it was stunning, but Tamsin was afraid to touch it, for fear of breaking it, never mind wearing it.

What if the clasp broke?

Wearing this one was out of the question. At just that moment, Ben appeared in the doorframe.

"Ah, Tamsin. Welcome! I see you are looking at one of ma-ma's favourites. The Ceylon Ruby. That was given to my great-great-great grandfather when he served in Myanmar and Sri Lanka, then called Ceylon. It was a true favourite of my mother's and she would be so pleased to see you wearing it."

At that, Tamsin decided it had to be the Ruby set.

"Come and meet Van," Ben said. "Van styles my clothes for events like this, and he also does hair, so he will do yours. He's brought his partner Maria to do your make-up. They will both need to see the dress and jewels you'll be wearing. Helen can show them that, while we have a drink."

They walked to the drawing room where more drinks awaited them.

"What would you like?" he asked.

"What's on offer? I've already had some of the champagne."

"Yes, I always keep a good amount on hand here, since Pepper abhors champagne."

Looking at the opulence of the home Ben lived in, Tamsin did not understand why he was going to leave Kensington to live in a draughty small cottage and open a restaurant in Oxford. Of course, he wouldn't be selling his

Kensington home, but it just didn't make sense to her. It seemed rude to ask, so she'd have to think of another way to put it that would not insult him.

In the meantime, they hardly knew anything about each other and it was time to find out. She was particularly curious about what Nico had told her.

"So Ben, will any of your ex-girlfriends be at the ball?" Tamsin asked, using the intel Nico had given her. It was shameful to use it, and she knew it, but she had to try to find out more about Caroline.

"Yes," he said, as he handed her another glass of champagne. "Both Clarissa Hodges and Caroline Martin will likely be there. Clarissa and I dated for a while, years ago, but it was never going to work out. We had nothing in common. She is now married to a Marquess. Given his status, they will both be there tonight. Caroline, I am not so sure about. She and I were in a long term relationship and, I may as well tell you, since it will come out soon enough, we were engaged to be married, but we ended things last winter."

He didn't seem to want to say more, so she left it there. Tamsin could not wait to see what both of the women looked like and what they would be wearing to the ball. Hopefully Caroline had moved on, was all Tamsin could think.

"Tamsin?" Van asked as he walked into the room, waiting to help her get ready.

"Yes," she said, handing her drink to Ben, as she got up and followed Van.

CHAPTER 40

The Ball

It took an hour, but by the time Tamsin's hair and make-up were done, she was unable to recognize herself. She was there, she knew, under the dazzling stones and make-up, and piles of velvet. She walked out into the hallway and Ben said, "Wow. You looked amazing in that dress at the boutique, but I had not realized how gorgeous you really are until this moment." He leaned in and gave her a kiss on the lips. Ben also looked amazing. He was wearing navy as well, which was the perfect complement to his blond hair.

"Ready?" he asked her.

"As I will be," she said.

"Ok, let's go." He took her hand and they walked down the front stairs of the house and into a different car this time, a Rolls Royce, which had a driver.

Tamsin's door was opened for her and she got in as carefully as she could, trying not to crush the dress.

She wondered how people could do this all the time. It would be exhausting.

But they didn't, did they? Even the King and Queen didn't get dressed up in this type of attire on a daily basis.

She was worried she was going to have a panic attack, and started to feel overwhelmed. That would be very embarrassing, especially since she hadn't told Ben that she had an anxiety problem. But when Ben got in next to her and held her hand, her nervousness faded away.

"So, what happens at a ball, Ben?" She asked because she had no idea.

"There will be drinks, then dinner, followed by dancing. A few speeches before we eat, although they should be short. My father will say something of course as the chair of the foundation. Think of this for what it is. A fundraising event for the charity."

"How much do tickets cost?"

"Oh," he chuckled. "Each table of eight starts at two hundred and fifty thousand pounds."

Tamsin shuddered. That meant her seat alone was worth over thirty thousand pounds. She hoped that by attending she wasn't taking a place that would otherwise have been paid for.

"Don't worry, Tamsin," Ben said, as if reading her mind. "I have paid for our seats, as is my duty. All members of the nobility who attend will contribute the minimum amount for one table, but most will give much more. It's the standard practice."

This was all getting to be too much for Tamsin, so she started to do some deep breathing, hoping Ben would not notice. It was to slow her heart rate down and relax. She'd been very good the last year or so at managing her anxiety, but these were surely special circumstances.

Anyone would be stressed out in this situation, wouldn't they?

They arrived at the Queen's House, Greenwich, where a long red carpet had been laid out for the guests. They entered from the front gates of the park, and walked a short distance to the front door of the Queen's House.

It was too cold to be outside this evening, but she thought it would be very pretty here in the summer. They had a lovely patio area outside, roped off by red velvet ribbons, and with a red carpet runway. There were several tall tables set up, for anyone who wanted or needed to get some air, she assumed.

Ben took her hand as she got out of the car and walked boldly ahead, ignoring the flashing cameras. People were calling out 'Harry' and it wasn't until they entered the building that Tamsin realized they were shouting to Ben. As soon as they walked into the venue, Tamsin felt like she was in a historical drama. Everyone and everything looked absolutely beautiful. There were hundreds of candles and there was a warm glow from the candlelight and dimly lit chandeliers. Everyone would look fab in this soft lighting, she thought.

They hadn't moved more than a few feet before people started coming up to Ben to say hello. She met so many people in the first ten minutes she couldn't remember anyone's name.

They broke free of people for a moment and stopped walking.

"Tamsin?" Ben asked her.

"Yes?"

"Over there at the bar is Caroline, my ex. She seems to be on her own at the moment but she is sure to have come with someone. I think it would be good for us to go and say hello to her now, so that we can move on and enjoy ourselves tonight. What do you think?"

"Um, ok. If you think that's the best way to manage things," Tamsin said.

She was worried about meeting anyone who knew Ben other than the people she had already met, like Giles, Suzie, Patrick, his father Charles, and Pepper. It would be easier for her if she only had to talk to them, but she knew that wouldn't be the case.

Just as they started to make a move, Giles appeared. He greeted her with a kiss on the cheek and shook Ben's hand.

"Oh, Giles," Ben said, "We were just going over to say hello to Caroline."

"I see," said Giles. "Good luck."

On their way to the bar, they ran into more people who knew Ben and stopped him to say hello. Ben kept introducing Tamsin to everyone, but all their names and titles started to meld together in her mind. She just smiled widely at everyone, nodded and said 'Hello' when Ben introduced her.

As they continued to be held up by people wanting to talk, all she could do was stare at Caroline as discreetly as possible, and try not to get caught. Caroline was blonde, like Ben. She had long, perfectly coiffed curls, obviously done just before the ball, and long red nails. She was wearing a dark green form hugging strapless dress, with a plunging neckline, and she had the perfect figure for a dress of this style, curvy where it counted. She was absolutely stunning and covered in diamonds. She sparkled like the stars in the sky.

Following Ben closely, and holding his hand, they

arrived at the bar, and Tamsin found she was facing Caroline straight on.

"Caroline, this is my girlfriend, Tamsin."

Caroline looked at Tamsin the way Pepper had when Ben said she was staying the night – with shock. Not wanting to betray her emotions, she formed a small smile, behind which Tamsin could tell she had gritted teeth.

"How nice for you, Ben."

"Well, just wanted to say hello. We're off," and at that, Ben ushered Tamsin away from Caroline.

"Sorry about that, Tamsin. But I just couldn't stand her smug look for one more moment. I didn't even let you speak, I was so irritated."

"It's ok. She didn't seem like she wanted to engage, frankly."

"No, and that's just her style. She doesn't really have feelings, Caroline, but now that we've said hello to her, she isn't likely to stare us down all evening. Let's go find Giles and get a drink."

Although he'd said that Caroline wouldn't be looking at them, Tamsin could feel her eyes laser focussed on their backs.

Before they got to Giles, who they could see across the room, Suzie and Patrick came up to say hello.

"Hi, Tamsin," they said in unison.

"Hello, Suzie, Patrick," she said, as she kissed them both on each cheek.

"You look enchanting," said Patrick.

"Very lovely indeed," said Suzie. "I see you are wearing the Ceylon Ruby," she said, leaning in close to whisper to Tamsin. "Ben must be over the moon seeing you wear that. It was his mother's favourite necklace."

"Yes, so I understand. It's incredibly beautiful," said Tamsin.

"Let's go sit down. We're at the same table tonight," said Suzie. "You can tell me where you got this stunning gown."

As they sat down side by side Suzie said, "I'm so glad you are here Tamsin. This annual event is quite important to Ben and his father and it's nice to see Ben happy and smiling."

Tamsin nodded as she scanned the room. She could see Ben talking to his father, and then he began to walk over to their table. Caroline caught him halfway, put her hand on his chest, said something and then Ben continued walking to their table.

"Are you enjoying yourself, Tamsin?" Ben asked when he arrived.

"Yes, very much. How is your father, and Pepper?"

"He's very pleased with the attendance and the press being here always helps raise the profile of the charity. I haven't seen Pepper, but I know she's here."

"What did Caroline want?"

"She wanted to ask me who you are, since she doesn't know you of course. But I told her I had to get back to you and left it at that."

He kissed her hand and was about to say something when the lights were dimmed further and his father took the podium.

After a series of short speeches, dinner was served.

Ben admired most of the dishes, and questioned a few choices the chef had made, but was generally favourable about the menu. Tamsin thought everything was delicious. Before the dancing began, Ben asked Tamsin to go outside with him to admire the view of Canary Wharf.

It was cold, but he put his arms around her as they looked across the river to the famous skyline. He was right, it was a beautiful sight.

"You haven't told me what you're going to call the restaurant, Ben. What will it be?" Tamsin asked.

"I'm not sure yet, but I need to choose soon, so I can register the name. I have two ideas. Selecting one word to convey the bounty of the land and the pureness of the food is really hard. Father has suggested I call it Tansley, but that seems a bit too focussed on me. I want it to be about the food. I'll sort it out. Have to, now that Gran has agreed the price of the building. I guess I should get the architect and builders involved soon. Do you want to help me with that, Tamsin?"

Much as she wanted to help Ben, she didn't have time to go to Oxford regularly. With university starting in a few weeks, possibly abroad, and moving as well, both of which she'd have to tell Ben about soon, there was little time left on top of work to do everything she needed, never mind help Ben get his restaurant fitted out.

"I'd be happy to, Ben, but the thing is, I have so much on right now. In fact, I wanted to tell you that..."

They were interrupted by Caroline, who came onto the balcony, flirting shamelessly and loudly with a tall, very handsome man. She laughed and stroked his chest with her long red nails. It was embarrassing to watch.

Ben looked over as he couldn't help but hear her giggle, turned back to Tamsin and said, "Let's go back inside."

She didn't want to ask who Caroline was with, since it

was obvious that even if Ben knew, he didn't want to talk about it.

❊ ❊ ❊

The night continued with dancing and they left just after eleven o'clock. Their car took them back to Ben's, which Tamsin had agreed to earlier in the night.

When they arrived, Tamsin was ready to kick off her heels and get out of the dress. As soon as she did, she felt so relieved to be free of the tight fitting garments. She pulled all of the pins out of her hair, and let it fall down over her shoulders, shaking her head and running her fingers through it to make it as light as possible.

On the bed lay a box with a ribbon. She opened it and inside found a stunning full length silk dressing gown in hunter green. She put it on, and reveled in the softness and luxuriousness of it.

Ben came into the bedroom, put his arm around her waist as she combed her hair, and pulled her in close to him, kissing her neck. She put the brush down and turned around to face him. He started to kiss her gently and playfully on the lips. She undid the silk tie around her waist, let the gown slide off her shoulders to the floor, and followed Ben to the bed. The passion he had for her was much more intense than the last time they were together, and she felt more for him with each day. They spent hours getting to know each other's bodies better, and then slowly fell asleep.

CHAPTER 41

Saturday 23rd November

In the morning, Tamsin woke again to the smell of fresh coffee. She put the silk robe on, went into the hall, and looked over the railing to the lower ground floor where the kitchen was.

She wanted coffee but didn't want to walk all the way down five floors. There was an elevator, but she didn't want to seem lazy taking it. Although, she was pretty tired. The ball and Ben had worn her out last night. She went back to brush her hair and find the slippers he had also bought for her. A few minutes later, Ben arrived with coffee and croissants and said, "The paps are out there."

"Paps? What are paps?"

Then Tamsin realized what Ben meant.

Paparazzi.

People waiting to take his photo, and probably hers.

"But why?" she asked, genuinely not understanding.

"I am on several of the 'most eligible bachelor' lists and they usually don't bother me, unless I am with a woman. Not that I am very often. But since I haven't been seen with a woman who isn't related to me in almost a year, apparently you being with me at the ball is news. Don't worry about it. Gary will make sure they leave, soon, but perhaps you'd like to keep away from the windows. Their cameras can capture details you would not believe."

Tamsin was a bit worried to hear this, but figured Ben would handle it, and she stepped away from the curtain and sat at the table by the wardrobe.

"So, did you have a good time last night?" Ben asked as he poured more coffee for Tamsin and leaned down to kiss her. His lips were soft and she could feel she was falling for him.

"I did. It was really lovely, Ben. Thank you for inviting me."

"Sorry that Caroline was hanging around so much. She just can't help herself."

He handed Tamsin a chocolate croissant and buttered some toast for her.

Tamsin wasn't sure this was the right time to ask about Ben's break-up with Caroline but she did want to know more about his past.

"Why did your engagement end?" she asked.

"The truth is that Caroline ran off with someone else. But the public story is that we just decided to go our own ways. In the end, her fling with the minor Swedish Royal she left me for did not last, but I guess she thought at the time that he was worth throwing away our lives together for. And based on last night, it looks like she's moved on from him as well. She has been trying to get me back all year to be straight about it, Tamsin. But I have finally let her out of my mind, and I'm not going back to her."

"That's good to hear," said Tamsin, although slightly worried about how Caroline behaved at the ball and what a spectacle she had made of herself, obviously trying to get Ben to notice her.

"What about you, Tamsin? I know absolutely nothing about your romantic past, other than you said you were in a long term relationship yourself."

"Yes, well, not much to tell, really. I had thought my partner Jason was the right man for me, and that we were on a path towards marriage and kids. But once he got what he was after, he left me for his secretary. It's so tiresome, I hate talking about it. I live in his flat, where we used to live together, and I have to move out next month, because he wants to sell it and buy a big house for his new wife. She is pregnant and due any time."

"That's a lot to tell, actually, Tamsin." Ben didn't really know what to say.

"It's ok."

"And where are you planning to move?"

"Well, I've found a place at Canary Wharf..." and she went on to tell him about the one decent flat she had seen.

"That sounds good. But isn't it a bit quiet over there?"

"Not really. There are lots of buildings going up and everyone is back at work now in the financial district, so there are lots of people there on weekdays."

They both got ready and decided to go out for a nice lunch nearby. Tamsin had enjoyed the meals they had eaten together so far, but Ben had not made dinner for her yet and she was really curious to find out what he would cook. He offered to do so next week, and she accepted. Tamsin knew she had to get home and work on her application for university in America, so after a delicious lunch at a place without photographers camped outside, she told Ben she had to go and he drove her home.

CHAPTER 42

Tamsin worked for a few hours filling in the online forms required for the University of Texas Law School application. When she finished, there was still one reference she needed and she sent an email to her old boss asking if he would provide her with one. There were only a few days left to submit the application, so she put reminders everywhere, pinging herself on WhatsApp and plastering post-it notes all over the flat to remind herself to chase the reference down every day of the week until it came in. This scholarship was the best chance she had to get to her dream of becoming a barrister, and to do so faster than any other route.

Tamsin knew it was time to tell her parents about the various things going on with her, so she called, hoping to catch them both in. On a Saturday afternoon, her father might be at the beach detectoring, or her parents could be out together taking a stroll, but it was worth a try. Her mum picked up and was thrilled to hear her voice.

"Tamsin! We haven't heard from you in almost a week. We were getting worried."

"Sorry, mum. I've just had a lot on and that's what I want to talk to you and dad about. Is he there?"

"Yes, dear. Let me get him. Martin?!" and she heard her

mother walking away from the phone and muffled voices in the background.

A moment later they both came on the line, using the speaker.

"Tamsin, it's dad. Is everything alright?"

"Oh, yes dad. Don't worry. I just wanted to talk to you and mum about a couple of things." She told them that she had sold four properties and they were thrilled to hear it.

"I am so proud of you, Tamsin," said her dad.

"I've also found a new flat, over at Canary Wharf."

"Aren't those very expensive?" her mum asked, sounding concerned. "Can you afford it?"

"I can now. But there is something else I want to talk to you both about."

"Go on dear," her mum said.

"Well, I've had an idea about going abroad for uni."

"What?" her father asked, as if he misheard what she said.

"You see, I found out that I can get a scholarship to the University of Texas Law School, all expenses paid, and I'm just sending in my application now."

"But..." Her mother was speechless for a moment.

"Aren't you going to City University in January, Tamsin?" asked her father.

"Well, that has been my plan. And it may still be what I do, but if I get accepted to the University of Texas, that might be the best option for me."

"Can you study law in America and then practice in the UK?" her father asked.

"Yes. There are a few things I'd have to do once I finish, but nothing too difficult."

"I see," said her mother, sounding very deflated at the news.

"So what about the flat you just mentioned you have found?" her father asked.

"Well, it is a bit of a balancing act right now, but I've worked it out. All letters of acceptance for the scholarship will be made by December fifteenth, which means I'd still have a few days before the fees for my term starting in January are due to City University. And I could decide whether I want to take the flat at that time." It sounded confusing, even to her, so it must be baffling her parents. "I mean, this flat in particular might be gone by then, but I could find something else before I come home to see you both for Christmas. That is, if I still need a flat. I won't if I'm going to Texas."

"Hmm," her father said, not sounding at all convinced that the timeline made sense, and probably worried now about Tamsin going abroad to study, especially since she had never before mentioned she was considering doing anything like that.

Not waiting for further feedback on her plan, Tamsin said, "I think I have all the main issues sorted out. What do you both think?"

"I don't know, Tamsin," her father said. "Have you ever been to Texas? What city is the university in?"

She went on to explain to them that it was in Austin and that no, she had never been to Texas, but she'd been doing some research and it looked great.

"Mum?" she asked, since her mother had not said anything.

"I didn't know you wanted to go away to study law, Tamsin."

"I didn't and I don't. But this may be the only way I can study full time. I mean, I'd have to quit my job, but since fees for law and housing would all be fully paid for, this is the opportunity of a lifetime. I'd be done in one year instead of two and then I can get back home and start working in law, which has always been my goal."

"Yes, we know, dear. But you could always just come and live at home with us and study full time, couldn't you?"

"Technically, yes. And I'm grateful to you both for offering me that option, I am. Not everyone has such amazing parents as you and dad, so I appreciate it. I could do that, but it would still be two years of study instead of one, and I just don't know. Let me see if I get accepted first, ok?"

"Ok, Tamsin. We support you whatever you want to do," her father said.

"Yes, we love you, dear. Whatever you want is fine with us. Just let us know."

Tamsin felt very guilty now for not telling them about Ben. But the timing was not right. She had already given them a lot to worry about already. Telling them about her new love interest could wait. And given how the conversation had gone, she also decided not to tell them about her plans to go to Carmel during Christmas. That would upset them for sure. Thinking about it now, she decided to check flights and hotels and book her trip if there was a good deal.

CHAPTER 43

Sunday 24th November

On Sunday, Tamsin thought she should write down all the pros and cons of everything she was trying to do, to find out what her head was telling her. Her heart was saying that she should go to Texas and take a week off in sunny Carmel.

But where did that leave her and Ben?

And what was really going on between them anyway?

This was just a fling, wasn't it?

She wasn't so sure anymore.

They'd spent two very sexy, incredible nights together, and she was letting her guard down more than she normally would. But since it wasn't serious, she didn't really worry. Ben would never consider marrying a woman like Tamsin. She was sure he was just having fun as well, and getting over his ex-fiancée fully by having a good time with someone else.

What was it about Tamsin that would prevent Ben from making this a serious relationship, at least as far as he was concerned? The answer was simple, really. She had no pedigree, and no money. End of story. Working class girls do not wind up with Viscounts, Duke and Lords. It was only by total chance that Tamsin had met Ben anyway, and even more by chance, or luck, or both, that she was working at the posh Red Brick Realty, where all the clients were millionaires.

No, this relationship was no more serious for Ben than it was for her. Even if he did invite her to a ball, and buy her a gown, and introduce her to all his father's friends, and even to his ex-fiancée, as his girlfriend.

Tamsin was sure that Ben wasn't serious about her.

And even if he was super handsome, incredibly fit, great in bed, funny, and charming, he wasn't what Tamsin needed right now. She had given up far too much for Jason and she would not do that again.

Tamsin was finally on the path to her destiny, and nothing was going to get in the way of that this time.

In fact, she thought, maybe she would have to make up excuses and decline all the invitations he had given her, including having dinner at Suzie and Patrick's, letting Ben cook her dinner this week, and the Christmas party at Tansley Hall. She'd sleep on it and see how she felt in the morning.

CHAPTER 44

Monday 25th November

On Monday morning, it seemed like everyone had been at a Christmas party all weekend and was still hung over when Tamsin walked into the office. No one was interested in doing anything. Sammy was the exception. He was chipper and had an update for Tamsin on Antony V and the Shoreditch flats.

Antony had been doing his part, but one of the sellers was dragging their feet. Sammy needed Tamsin to call them because they were ignoring him. Given Antony V had started inviting people to his private, exclusive New Year's Eve party, being held in both flats, the deal had to go through. He also needed time to knock through the wall between them. And of course, the sales had to go through for Tamsin as well, since she was borrowing money from Becca to secure a new flat for herself and getting an advance at work, all on the basis of the flats selling.

Tamsin was just about to call the seller of the flat who was not doing what they needed to, after getting off the phone with Antony V, when Lily called her to say that Lord Tansley was at the front desk for her.

Oh my GOD!

What was Ben's Father doing here?

Or wait, could it be Ben downstairs?

If it was Ben, did he actually tell the receptionist he was a Lord?

That wasn't really Ben's style.

"Thank you, Lily. Be right down," was all Tamsin could say.

She practically flew down the staircase, and, walking quickly over to Ben, said, "Hi Ben, nice to see you."

He responded by leaning in and giving her a kiss on the lips. Everyone turned their heads, since by now, Lily had instant messaged the entire office through the group channel that Lord Tansley was on the premises and here to see Tamsin.

"Do you have a few minutes to talk?" he asked, holding both her hands.

Tamsin looked over her shoulder and saw that everyone in the open plan space was looking at her and Ben, but pretending to be busy doing something else. Ben was completely oblivious to this.

"Um, well, I..."

"Lord Tansley," said a voice suddenly behind Tamsin.

She jumped. Then she turned and saw that it was James. He stuck out his hand to shake Ben's.

"Ben, please."

James just nodded at this.

"I'm James Tomkin. Welcome to Red Brick Realty. I understand Tamsin has been helping you with your property search in Oxford."

And a lot more than that! thought Tamsin, knowing everyone else was thinking the same thing.

"Yes, she's been marvellous. I've just dropped in to see if Tamsin can spare me a moment or two to discuss the architectural ideas for my new restaurant, since I was passing by."

"Of COURSE! Tamsin, get your coat," James said.

And she did as directed, wanting to shrink under a desk and disappear, knowing that by now, everyone knew that she and Ben were an item.

As she passed the photocopier to get her coat, she saw the front cover of one of the dailies that had been left on top, which had a photo of Ben and the headline '*New Love for Lord T!*'

CHAPTER 45

"Did you introduce yourself as Lord Tansley?" Tamsin asked Ben when they got outside.

"No." He seemed confused "Why?"

"Oh nothing. But have you seen the cover of today's dailies?"

"No, I ignore those like the plague."

"The cover of one said something about a 'New love for Lord T' or similar."

Ben laughed.

"They are so ridiculous. Honestly. Whoever runs those papers and agrees to the headlines is beyond me. We don't really engage with the press that carries such nonsense."

"So, I should...?"

"Ignore it, entirely. They make their money off salacious material. The slightest hint that me or anyone in a position like mine has anything going on in their lives that the public would like to know about is just pound signs to them."

"I see."

"What was the photo, did you notice?"

"Looked like an old photo of you."

"Exactly. They didn't get any photos of us on Saturday morning when you were at my house, and they had left by the time we went out, so the next photos, probably in tomorrow's paper, will be of us at the ball. They will have figured out we were together."

"*Next* photos?"

Tamsin realized she hadn't told her parents about Ben yet, and now they might see these stories too. She'd have to call her mum later. But the bigger issue was that all her colleagues now knew about her and Ben.

She realized she hadn't told James that she and Ben were becoming friends, never mind lovers. That of course wasn't his business, but she wondered if she was breaking some sort of work policy, dating a client.

She'd thought about mentioning it casually the other day, but it had slipped her mind, and she hadn't mentioned it to him. James would never believe her now if she said she and Ben were just friends. Especially not if photos of them at the ball came out. She hoped she wouldn't lose her job.

"So, what is it you wanted to ask me about?"

They were at the pub on the corner, being as incognito as possible.

"Right, well..." and he explained plans that the architect had proposed to him earlier that day. He could have emailed them to her, so clearly Ben wanted to see her.

Tamsin didn't like having to be picture perfect ready to see him at any time, and was now feeling self-conscious about their relationship.

Before, she didn't care about wearing slouchy jeans and tops, as long as she wasn't seeing clients.

But now, it seemed she should smarten herself up a bit, especially if the paparazzi could be around at any time.

This was more than Tamsin had bargained for when she went to bed with Ben.

"Look, Ben, I need to tell you something," she said, cutting him off mid-sentence.

"Ok. Sounds important."

"It is. I am not looking for a relationship, which I think I told you before. Or at least, if I didn't, I meant to. Anyway, I am about to go back to uni to become a barrister and I thought we were just having fun, but it seems that now, things are getting outside of our control."

"I see." He was silent for a moment. "Yes, you did tell me that you were not looking for a relationship, and neither was I. However, I thought that we had something special happening here, Tamsin. Whether we wanted it or not. I mean, I don't just jump into bed with any woman I meet. You've seen how the press behave. I can't afford to do that, for my sake or any woman's. They are ruthless and they will crush anyone without a second thought. Is it the press that's causing you concern?"

"No, and yes. I mean, it's not nice to think that they are following us around and taking pictures. But it's more that I have a plan for my life and there aren't any men in it. At least, not until I get where I am going, which is becoming a barrister. That dream has been thwarted once already, by a man, and I'm not letting that happen again. I'm sorry to tell you this here, like this, without any warning, but I knew I had to do it soon.

"And," Tamsin continued, "You may as well also know at this point that I might be going to America to finish my studies, starting in January."

"January? So soon."

"Yes. So perhaps, Ben, us spending more time together is just not worth it. I mean, not worth, I just mean, may not be a good idea, since I am likely leaving town in a few weeks, for at least a year, maybe longer."

Why she was telling him all of this now, when she hadn't even put in the application for university yet, was unclear to Tamsin. But she had started to let him know about her goals and she didn't want to stop.

"Look, I have to go. I have a major sale in the works that I need to sort out, so I have to get back to the office."

"Will you still come for dinner?"

"I don't know. I need to think." She left him in the pub and walked back to work.

Before going in, she stopped at a news stand and saw several covers of different papers with Ben's face on the front page and multiple headlines questioning who his new love interest was. She dreaded tomorrow's papers, which, if Ben was right, would have photos of them both on page one.

She decided to call her parents to warn them about this.

"Mum?"

"Yes, Tamsin?"

"Tomorrow there are going to be papers with my face on the front cover."

"Whatever for, dear?"

"I've been working with a client named Lord Tansley, and we went to a ball together on Friday night. This is now news to the gossip papers and I wanted to let you know, so you are not alarmed. If anyone asks, just tell them that he is a client of mine. Or tell them nothing, if you can."

"Ok, dear."

"And tell dad too."

"Is there anything to worry about?"

"No, but I expect this to carry on for a few days, that's all."

CHAPTER 46

Tuesday 26th November

As expected, all covers of the daily gossip sheets had a photo of Tamsin and Ben on the front page. Headlines included 'Who is this mystery woman?' and 'Estate agent the new Lady T?'

All Tamsin could think was she was glad she'd warned her parents.

Becca called her at seven o'clock as she was getting ready for work.

"Uh-oh," said Becca when Tamsin picked up.

"Yeah."

"How bad is it?"

"Bad. He came to my work yesterday and everyone had seen the papers by then, except me. Not sure how I can go in and face everyone at the office today."

"You'll be fine. Who cares what anyone thinks?"

"I wish it were that easy, Becca."

"It is. Just forget about everyone else."

"The problem is bigger than that. I thought we were just having fun. But then, well, I wasn't so sure. I was starting to fall for his boyish charm. But I am NOT getting forced off my plans again, Becca. I haven't even told you – I've applied to go to uni in the US. I'll know in three weeks if I get the scholarship. So I won't borrow that money just yet, either, as I'm not taking a new flat. At least, not right now."

Tamsin gathered her things for the office but was distracted by all the items swirling in her mind. Ben had invited her for a meal this week, and they were supposed to be going to Suzie and Patrick's house on Saturday for dinner, but at the moment, Tamsin didn't feel in the mood to do anything with Ben, or with anyone he knew.

She had tried to book her trip to Carmel, but her card kept getting rejected, as if it was a sign that she shouldn't go. She'd try again later, because she had decided she was taking a trip to Carmel, no matter what.

The estate agent for the flat in Millharbour had called her twice yesterday, and she knew she should get back to him, but she still wasn't sure what to say.

She pulled the sticky note off the fridge, crumpled it up and tossed it in the bin, since the last reference she needed for the scholarship application had come through an hour earlier.

As she finished her coffee, she uploaded the reference into her application for the University of Texas, which was now complete, three days before the final deadline, and she locked the front door.

CHAPTER 47

Walking along Kings Road, Tamsin wondered what she was going to do. Everyone at work knew she had been seeing Ben. That was obvious. Why it bothered her so much, she wasn't sure. Maybe it was because it felt like they had been laughing at her behind her back. As if the idea of her going out with a Viscount was a joke. They were probably jealous, or she was being paranoid, or both. She couldn't think straight.

She was overreacting, she knew, and doing so often led to anxiety attacks, so she tried to slow her breathing down, using breathing cycles of four. Having that second coffee this morning was a mistake. She was wired and ready to snap.

She entered the turnstile on the main floor of her office building and then the elevator, not seeing anyone. When the elevator opened at her office floor, Lily said, "Hi, Tamsin. James wants to see you."

Continuing past Lily's desk, she dropped her things on her own and headed to the bathroom, where she needed a moment to get herself together. She pinched her cheeks, since she looked pale, and then walked to James's office, ready for whatever he had to say. She knocked and he answered the door with a broad smile.

"Tamsin, you dark horse!"

What is he saying? she wondered.

She thought he was going to fire her.

"Going out with a Viscount, and not even telling us! What else are you hiding?"

Now she understood. It seemed James loved her new-found fame for the free PR this would give to Red Brick Realty.

"I was going to tell you, since he's a client, but I've been so busy and I didn't see you for a few days…"

"It's alright, perfectly alright. How good to have him and his grandmother as clients. I didn't realize that those trips to Oxford were to help the Smythe-Joneses."

"They weren't trips to help them. They were to sell the cottage, at least at first, and then…"

"Never mind that now, Tamsin. Come in and tell me what you and Viscount Tansley have been up to."

Tamsin was not at all comfortable with this conversation. Everyone knew she and Ben had been at a ball on Friday night. What else was there to say?

"What do you mean, sir?"

"Well, are you a couple? You went to a major society event with him, so it has to be serious. Look!"

He handed her the daily paper, on which she and Ben were the only story on the front page. There was a photo of them walking to the Queen's House, holding hands.

"No, sir, not really. We're just casually acquainted."

"Nonsense. But if you want to keep it to yourself, that's fine with me. How are the Viscount's property purchases going?"

"Fine, sir. I meant to ask you how or why Mr. Crighton

took the offer on Lavender Cottage at the price he did. Did you persuade him?"

"That wasn't necessary. I think he'd had enough of dealing with the place, and just wanted to move on. He's getting a very good price for it, so he should be happy. And it's cash as well."

"Yes."

Feeling as though the discussion was over, Tamsin moved to leave.

"Davies?"

"Yes?"

"You will make sure these deals go through smoothly, right?"

"Of course, sir."

When she got to her desk, her phone was ringing. It was Andrew. He'd no doubt seen the news.

"Hi, Andrew."

"Tamsin! What *have* you been doing? I leave for a week, and chaos ensues."

"Can't talk now, Andrew. At work."

"Ok, I get it. You look *marvellous* on the covers today, Tamsin. But where did you get that dress?!"

"I think you can guess."

"Oh yes, I am sure I can. *Lord Tansley*. Are you free later, now I'm back in town?"

It was only ten o'clock, but Tamsin was already looking forward to a drink, and asked Andrew to meet her after work. She quickly identified a quiet pub she'd never been to nearby on Google, where hopefully no one would recognize her.

CHAPTER 48

Having successfully dodged the estate agent wanting to know if she was going to take the flat, Tamsin left the office a bit early. All day it seemed that she could do no wrong, at least in James's view. She hurried through the windy rain to the Hare and Toad pub, and found a quiet respite from the nasty weather outside.

Andrew arrived a moment later, after she had found a table and taken off her coat.

"What will it be, Cherie?" he asked while leaning in to kiss her on each cheek.

"Large white wine. Thanks, Andrew."

Her hair was a mess. It fell far past her shoulders, and really needed to be tied up in weather this foul, but she'd forgotten anything to hold it at the office. She smoothed it down as best she could, before Andrew returned.

"Cheers!" they said as they clinked glasses.

"So good to see you, Tamsin. Where did you meet the Viscount?"

Andrew could not contain his excitement, having been a lifelong fan of the royal family. He had some ancient aristocratic connections himself, which he never tired of telling people he just met.

"Tell me about Milan first."

"Had fun. Spent loads. Now dish."

She explained how she'd met Ben, the confusion over his given name, and stayed light on details.

"Let me get this straight. You like him, he's great in bed, he's gorgeous, and rich, and yet, you don't want to see him anymore. Is that right?"

"About right."

"And that's because…?"

"Like I said, I need to get myself organized, Andrew. I am going back to finish law. I am becoming a barrister, and that's it. *Nothing* is going to get in the way of that now."

"Can't you do both?"

"How?"

"I don't know. Go to uni part time, move to a new flat and keep seeing the Viscount?"

"That will never work."

"Why not?"

"Because."

But Tamsin could not think of a single good reason why Andrew's suggestion would not work. She had been round and round the options in her head hundreds of times and had already thought of his idea herself. The only solution was to go to America.

And if that didn't work out for whatever reason, then she was moving home to Margate, quitting her job and studying full time. There would be no time for men in any scenario that saw her becoming a barrister.

Andrew told her more about his work trip to Milan and after another drink they decided to leave.

"Excuse me," said the bartender as Tamsin passed by on her way out. "Is this you?" he pointed to the photo in the paper.

"No, it's my twin."

CHAPTER 49

It was rare, but Tamsin was feeling really low when she got home. The kind of low that made her need something in her life to cuddle. Like a cat, or a dog. Something she could engage with, other than her mind.

She flipped the channels, trying to find something good to watch, had a peanut butter sandwich, being too lazy to make anything else, and headed to bed.

At eleven o'clock, the doorbell rang just as she was just drifting off to sleep.

It rang again and she went to look at the video cam. It was Jason.

She pressed the speaker and said, "Not now, Jason."

He kept ringing the bell.

What did he want this time?

Tamsin was very upset now that he'd woken her up and that he had come over at all, when she'd told him to stay away.

"What do you want, Jason?"

"Tams. Please let me in. I really need to talk to you."

Realizing he would not go away unless she let him in first, and worried about how he sounded, she reluctantly opened the door.

He walked in and went to pour himself a drink immediately.

"What is it?"

Jason moved to the couch, sat down and stared straight ahead.

"What, Jason?"

"I'm a dad, Tams. A dad." He took another swig of the whiskey.

"Congratulations. I'm happy for you. Now, can I go to back to bed?"

"This is awful, Tams. Awful."

"What's awful?"

"I'm not suited for it. I'm not right for being a father. I can't keep it together, Tams."

"Just calm down, Jason. It's ok. Come on. Have a little more whiskey to steady your nerves." She poured him a small amount and sat down with a glass of water for herself. Jason was trembling. She'd never seen him so upset in their years together.

"I saw you today. In the paper. Good for you, Tams. A Viscount. Good for you."

Worried about how he was acting, Tamsin put her hand on his arm, and he burst into tears.

"I'm sorry, Tams. I'm sorry." He kept repeating it over and over.

"It's ok, Jason. I have forgiven you, ok? Please stop crying."

Jason went to the bathroom and when he returned, he was more composed.

"Tamsin, I did you wrong. I know that now. I mean, I really know it. I blew it and we had something really special. You did everything for me, helped me get where I am professionally, which is where you want to be, and I took you for granted. You deserve the best, Tamsin. Maybe Viscount Tansley can give that to you. I know I can't. I have no idea how I am going to be a father or how to be a good husband."

"You will be fine, Jason. But maybe you should talk to someone so you can work through things, and give yourself the best chance of succeeding at both. What do you think?"

"Probably. Yes."

After another hour of consoling Jason and congratulating him again on becoming a father, she called him a cab and sent him home. She had him text his wife so she would know he was on his way.

Exhausted, she fell asleep with the lights on.

CHAPTER 50

Wednesday 27th November

Tamsin woke up feeling refreshed, and confident that she knew what to do. She'd behaved like a child towards Ben, and she would put things right. He was expecting her for dinner tonight so she would just show up and surprise him, since she'd been unclear about whether she was coming and if things were on or off between them.

When she went to his house at six o'clock, she buzzed as usual. Gary answered and she recognized his voice.

"Mistress Davies. One moment please."

Ben came to the speaker and said, "Tamsin, I wasn't expecting you."

In the background she could hear a woman's voice asking who it was.

"Nothing to worry about," he said to whoever had asked.

"Is this a bad time, Ben? You invited me to dinner tonight, so here I am."

"Yes, but, after our last discussion, when you said you needed to think things over, I wasn't expecting to hear from you for a while."

"Do you have company?"

"Yes, well, it's awkward, but Caroline is here."

CAROLINE. EX-FIANCÉE.

Tamsin turned and walked away as quickly as she could, hearing Ben calling her name through the speaker as she did.

CHAPTER 51

Thursday 28th November

Nico called her after work and asked how it had gone at the ball and how she was coping with the paparazzi.

"Ha, that's all done with, Nico. You were right about Caroline. She's awful."

Nico told her that Ben had been to the club last night, alone, and looked out of sorts.

"Ben only had a couple of drinks and then he left. It's not unusual for members to come on their own, but he looked very miserable."

And so he should, Tamsin thought.

"Considering how much Caroline still obviously wants him back, I'm not sure what he was bothered about."

"Aren't you two going out?"

"Not anymore. I went to his house for dinner last night, as agreed, only to find *you know who* there."

"Caroline?"

"Yes, and I didn't wait to find out why."

"He might have a very simple explanation for that. Did you ask him what she was doing there?"

"No. I just left."

"I think you should call him, Tamsin. Ring him up and

find out why Caroline was there. If he'd wanted to hide it, he could have done so."

True, thought Tamsin.

"Maybe I will call him. Later. But I've got a lot of other priorities right now."

"What about the flats we saw? Are you taking the one in Millharbour?"

"Not sure."

"I thought you loved it."

"I did. I do. But…"

She told him about the University of Texas application and that she wasn't sure she should get a flat until the answer from them was known. Nico said that made sense and agreed to tell Tamsin if Ben showed up with Caroline at the club.

Tamsin wasn't used to feeling sorry for herself. It was making her tired, being down. So she thought she'd take Nico's advice and call Ben to ask him what Caroline had been doing at his house before making any further judgements about the situation.

"Hello, Tamsin," Ben said when he picked up.

"Hi, Ben. Sorry I ran off like that, but it was a shock to hear that Caroline was at your place. What was she doing there anyway?"

"Trying her old tricks. She told Gary she needed to get something she couldn't find at her place, and must have left at my house. But that was just a ruse. He let her in, of course. Then you arrived about five minutes later and disappeared as quickly as you had come."

"Sorry, again, for that. It was childish."

"Don't worry about it. I might have reacted the same if

it were me. Anyway, are you still coming with me up to Suzie and Patrick's on Saturday? I need to let them know."

Tamsin considered this for a moment. If she said yes, she'd be back seeing Ben again, and that had a lot of pitfalls, and if she said no, then it was probably over with him. She wasn't sure about the first option, but was sure she didn't want the latter, no matter what her head was telling her.

"Yes, I'm looking forward to seeing them both and their farm."

"That's great, Tamsin. I'll pick you up at nine o'clock if that's ok. If you want, we can go to Tansley Hall afterwards. It would be a lot easier on me if we could stay over."

"Of course. I'd love to. Actually, have you ever had Ethiopian food? There's a place in Oxford I want to try out."

They agreed that on Sunday they would go for a punt on the river and try out the Ethiopian restaurant before heading back to London.

Tamsin wondered why she had worried about Caroline at all. It would be the same if Ben worried about Jason; unnecessary. Ben was a decent man and he'd been up front about everything to do with Caroline so far. Maybe Caroline wanted him back, but it was obvious to Tamsin that Ben didn't want anything more to do with his ex. At least that was one less thing to worry about.

CHAPTER 52

Saturday 30th November

On the drive to Oxford, Ben took a call from his father. They would need to stop by the Hall at some point before the end of the day, and decided to go there first. Ben's father had to give him some legal documents for the purchase of the building.

They stopped by the building on the river as well, and peered through the window. Ben slid the papers through the letter box at his solicitor's office in town and they got back on the road.

Tamsin wondered what the building should be called. Ben had not yet chosen a name for the restaurant and it felt awkward referring to its future location as 'The Building' all the time.

"How about giving the restaurant building a name?" she suggested.

"Ok, such as?"

"How about Cherwell, after the river?"

"I like it. 'Cherwell' it is."

They drove three miles out of Oxford to get to Honeychurch Farm, which Suzie and Patrick had revitalized as an organic farm over the last five years. Giles had

helped them by recommending new crop rotations and different ways to grow food.

Today Patrick wanted to get Ben's advice about something to do with grains he was growing that weren't turning out as they should. If that crop failed, he'd need another if he were going to supply Giles and Ben with bread on a daily basis.

The idea was that much of Patrick and Suzie's produce would be used in the new restaurant. They had over two hundred and fifty acres and it was a lot to look after on their own, so they had hired someone to manage and run it day-to-day. But there was still a lot for them to do, and the risk was all theirs.

Arriving on time, Ben drove up in front of the old, but tastefully restored eighteenth century farm house and rang the bell. Suzie opened the door and welcomed them both in. Tamsin could smell bread baking and craved toast with jam all of a sudden. She and Ben followed Suzie to the kitchen, where they found Patrick reading, and they said hello.

"So happy you two could make it," he said, putting down the paper. "I'm glad it's not raining!"

"Thanks for having us. It wasn't a bad journey. We missed a lot of traffic by leaving early," Ben said as he and Patrick wandered off to the back garden.

"Did you have a good time at the ball, Tamsin?" Suzie asked as she cleared the table and gestured for Tamsin to sit down.

"Yes, I did."

"I assume you have been unimpressed with how the press is treating you and Ben at the moment."

"Yes, it's been awful seeing myself on the front pages of all these papers. I was shocked and my parents and friends were as well. It was only a single evening. It's not like we are getting married."

"They can't help themselves. Honestly. It's a shame how aggressive they are. You can't let it get to you. If you go out with Ben, they will follow you and try to get your photo any time they can."

"Any advice? In case they do continue to pester me?"

"I'd say, don't hide from them, or try to cover your face, but don't talk to them either. It will just encourage them to keep after you. And whatever you do, ignore social media. No matter how fabulous you look, people will still criticize you online."

"Alright, thanks for the advice, Suzie." Tamsin looked over at what Suzie was making. "Delicious looking pie."

"Apple, given the time of year. Hope you enjoy it."

Suzie told her about the farm and how they had bought it from a family who had owned and run it for six generations. Now they were growing a variety of things that Ben and Giles were looking forward to using in the spring on their first menu, like runner beans and garlic.

"How is the restaurant purchase going?" asked Suzie.

"Fine. I believe that Ben has it all underway now. He might even get the keys before the new year."

"That would be wonderful. I know he has big plans for the restaurant. As does Giles, and as do we. Are you much of a foodie, Tamsin?"

"Not really. I mean, I love food, and I am partial to spicy dishes, but I'm not a connoisseur of any type of food."

"Has Ben made you dinner yet?"

"No, but he has made me some delicious breakfast, so I know he can cook." She wondered if that was saying too much about her and Ben, since making breakfast for her clearly indicated they had spent a night together, but Tamsin didn't want to hide anything about her relationship with Ben, at least not from his closest friends.

"What are your plans for New Year's Eve this year, Tamsin?"

"I don't have any yet," she lied.

Antony V had invited her to his party and wasn't taking no for an answer. He said it was all down to her that the party was even possible. While that might be partly true, she didn't think his type of bash was something she'd enjoy. Everyone would be twenty-five or younger, and she thought it unlikely Ben would go with her.

She'd asked Antony to invite Sammy instead. It was much more his kind of thing than her. He and Lily had hit it off and were secretly seeing each other, although it was obvious to everyone in the office, so Tamsin suggested Antony invite the two of them, knowing they would have a great time. He had agreed to that, but was still expecting her to show up. However, she had plans to be on the beach in Carmel on New Year's Eve.

"We are going to the Shard, if you'd like to join us. My father and his wife are celebrating their tenth wedding anniversary on the second of January. So Patrick and I are spending a few nights in London at our flat in Bloomsbury, and my father is hosting a party at the Shard on December thirty-first for friends and family. You are very welcome to join us for dinner and ring in the New Year if you can make it."

"That's very generous of you, Suzie."

Tamsin did not want to mention her plans for Carmel, which were yet to be confirmed, and because she hadn't told her parents or Ben about them yet.

"I'm going to be at my parents for Christmas in Margate, and haven't decided yet when I'm going back to London. Can I let you know soon?"

"Of course," said Suzie as she pulled the bread out of the oven and offered Tamsin a slice with butter. "Ben will be coming, as will Giles."

Tamsin didn't know if Giles was single but she thought so. She'd have to ask Ben later. Time was moving so fast and there was so much going on that Tamsin hadn't even met Ben's friend Gideon, who he often stayed with when he was in Oxford if he didn't want to be at Tansley Hall.

Although Ben had several rooms at the Hall, he'd told her that it was his father's house and that Pepper didn't always make him feel welcome there, which was why buying Lavender Cottage was a good idea. When he moved in there, he'd have his own home base in Oxford.

They decided to head outside to see what Patrick and Ben were up to. It was getting cold, so they bundled up and put their wellies on. Tamsin had almost forgotten to bring hers, but Ben reminded her it might be wet and would definitely be muddy. An Irish Terrier was patiently waiting at the door, along with a black cat, both desperate to go outside.

Suzie and Tamsin let the animals out and walked for a short while to the first field, where they used the two-way radio to call Patrick. Hearing that he and Ben would not be back for at least an hour, they went into the cold storage room in the barn and picked up yogurt and milk before heading back into the house.

In addition to growing vegetables, Suzie and Patrick also made the most delicious dairy products. Suzie offered Tamsin some cheese to try and she could not get enough. They gathered all the food into a basket and took it to the kitchen.

"Did Caroline disturb you at the ball?" Suzie asked when they got inside.

It had come out of nowhere, but Tamsin knew she'd have to reply.

"No. She barely spoke to either of us." She kept her voice as casual and light as she could.

"Caroline is a unique person. She is, as you would have seen yourself, incredibly beautiful and desirable to virtually every man alive. But she can never seem to settle down. Even when she says that's what she wants. We worried when Ben told us they were engaged, and our fears came true in the end. I suspect she might try to hang around a little, now that she has seen you. But just ignore her and any press attention it brings. Ben and Caroline were never meant to be."

Tamsin stayed quiet on hearing this, and filed the comment away. She didn't really want to find out more about Caroline, just like she didn't want to talk any further about Jason. They should both stay where they belonged – in the past.

"Ready for dinner!" yelled Patrick as he and Ben returned from the field.

"What are we having?" Ben asked.

"I've made Beef Wellington, with apple pie for dessert," said Suzie.

"Scrumptious," he replied.

They sat down to eat and talked about the ball and the upcoming plans for Christmas, the party at Tansley Hall and some of the menu items that Ben and Giles had been considering, running through the pros and cons of each.

After the meal, Ben and Tamsin said they would be heading to the Hall for the night. Suzie handed Tamsin the basket full of cheese and yogurt they had packed earlier, and she and Patrick waved them off and went indoors.

CHAPTER 53

Amore? Andante? Allegro?

Tamsin was trying but could not remember the restaurant name Ben was considering as the front runner. None of these, that was for sure.

Piquante.

That was it, the name he wanted for the restaurant. It didn't start with the letter 'A' at all. The other one he was considering was 'Seed & Soil'.

Tamsin didn't really like either of these options, but was sure that Ben would make the right choice. He was keen to get the name registered and start the advertising, although Tamsin thought it was far too early for that. He didn't own the building yet.

"Are you fixed on 'Piquante' for the restaurant name, or is it going to be something else?" Tamsin asked Ben as he drove towards Tansley Hall.

"I don't know. I like Piquante best, but I've been thinking about changing it. Given Davina says I need to consider social media in the name choice, I asked her to do her magic and give me some ideas next week."

Davina was Ben's friend from childhood and would be the brand manager for the restaurant, handling all the marketing, social media and PR as part of her client portfolio. It seemed that she was already busy doing what she could, but waiting on Ben to confirm the name.

Tamsin hoped the building sale went through before the end of the year and that Ben didn't waste too much time or money on something that was not for certain. She'd already told him this once and didn't want to remind him about it. Getting too excited this early could be a mistake.

"I've come up with a new name," he said. "It's 'Bimi'. What do you think?"

"What does it mean?"

"It's one word for 'delicious', in Japanese."

"I like it," she said. "Of the names you've mentioned, it sounds the nicest, and I think the back story of what it means in Japanese is interesting. I'm not a brand expert, but I think Davina can do more with it than with any of the other names you have considered."

"That's what I was thinking. It's short and sweet. Granny is not keen on the name 'Bimi', but Pepper and Father think it will do. I need something that inspires me and also excites the public enough to try the restaurant."

"What does Giles think?"

"He's behind it. Either that or Piquante. I'm just worried that might sound too spicy, and turn people off. Whereas, most people will not know what Bimi means."

"Agreed."

Tamsin changed the topic as they continued the drive to Tansley Hall.

"Suzie invited me to her father's New Year's Eve party at the Shard."

"That was nice of her. I was going to ask you to join me for that."

"I'm not sure I can make it. I'll be at my parents that week, and possibly in Carmel."

She had said it and was pleased for having done so.

"Carmel?" he asked, with some curiosity.

"Yes, I'm planning a few days there after Christmas, before I start uni."

He didn't press her on this, but he was curious to know why she was going to California.

"How did the flat hunting go? I forgot to ask."

"I found a good place at Millharbour, but I'm undecided. I'll think it over and make up my mind soon."

She wasn't ready to tell him about the University of Texas yet.

When they got to the Hall, Ben asked if Tamsin wanted to join him in his rooms, but she said she needed an early night.

As she entered her room, which was the Marlowe Suite again, she found that Helen had been in and turned down the bed, leaving some marzipan chocolate, and a new silk robe and slippers for her. Thinking she could get used to this pampering but trying to stay focussed on her plans, she opened the chocolate, drank a glass of the champagne which was chilling by the bed, and booked the most luxurious trip she could afford to Carmel, California, leaving on the twenty-ninth of December.

Now all she had to do was get the scholarship, and she'd be on her way to finally becoming a barrister. She found an old episode of Kavanagh QC online and watched it from bed, cosy under the covers, and then dozed off.

CHAPTER 54

Sunday 1st December

When Tamsin came downstairs, she found Pepper in the breakfast room alone. Feeling awkward, since she hadn't spoken more than a few words to Pepper, she said hello, helped herself to some food and sat down.

"I understand you are helping Ben with his restaurant," said Pepper.

Tamsin wasn't sure if it was a question or a statement and had no idea how to respond.

"Yes."

Silence. Tamsin continued eating.

"And what did you think of your dress? Felipe told me that you found it at Civello."

What didn't *Pepper know?* she wondered.

"I did, yes. It's extremely beautiful."

She wasn't sure what to talk about with Pepper, who was reading the paper, although it looked more like she was trying to ignore Tamsin.

"Do you ride, Tamsin?"

"No."

"Ben is out riding with his father. He'll be back soon.

Don't let me keep you," Pepper said, looking at Tamsin's empty plate.

Tamsin felt unwelcome and went to her room, messaging Ben to let him know where to find her when he returned.

"Yes?" Tamsin said to a knock at the door.

"It's me, Ben."

"Come in, Ben."

She told him about the encounter with Pepper.

"Don't worry about Pepper," he said as he gave her a kiss.

His cheeks were red and his face felt cool against her skin. Not knowing how to ride a horse was not something Tamsin had ever thought about, but now she wished she knew how so she could ride with Ben.

The size of the estate was large enough for hours of riding on a daily basis. For a moment, she wobbled, as she felt daunted by dating the future Earl of Tansley. The feeling passed and she reminded herself that she was only having fun and so was Ben. For now, that was all that mattered.

"She is just trying to figure out who you are. Since you are not part of her social circle, she has no idea what you like or what you have in common, other than what you or I tell her. I can share some basic things about her with you so that you have conversation starters when you see her. Same for my father as well, although he is easier to talk to. Shall we get going to take the punt and have lunch? I'm hungry after that ride."

"Yes, let's go!" she said and packed up her overnight bag.

❄ ❄ ❄

Luckily, Tamsin thought, the weather was nice. No rain in sight and just warm enough to take a punt on the river. They chose a boat and Ben paid for the ride. It was smoother than she thought it would be, but breezy. Ben wrapped his arms around her, and asked if she was having a good time.

"I am."

After the ride was done, they walked up the river bank to the Ethiopian restaurant, Aksum. Not knowing what to order, Tamsin read the entire menu twice, and landed on some vegetarian dishes, which they paired with beef. The interior of the restaurant was dark and quiet and they had timed their visit perfectly, just after the lunch crowd.

Tamsin didn't know that you could sit on the floor in this restaurant, and she thought that would be fun to try next time, as she looked at other people nearby dining this way. The hostess had simply offered them a table.

Ben told her about his plans to refurbish Cherwell and wanted her help with the architects and choosing countertops, furniture, paint and tile colours. It felt like a big commitment, of time, and also investment of herself in his life, since the restaurant meant a lot to him.

But not wanting to offend him, she said, "I may be able to help out one day this week, Ben," and changed the subject.

The food was delicious and as much fun as Tamsin imagined eating it would be. She was tired after such a big weekend and wanted to get home. Ben dropped her off when they got back to London, and carried on to his house in Kensington.

CHAPTER 55

Becca called Tamsin in the evening.

"What is *going on* with you?" Becca asked. "*All* week, photos of you in that incredible dress have been popping up on my mobile phone. I know I read too much trashy stuff, but you and Ben are everywhere."

"Yes, it's been a strange week," Tamsin reflected. "I'm going home for Christmas, as usual, but then I'm off to Carmel for a few days and I have to let my parents know, today. I can't leave it any longer."

"I don't envy you that conversation. Your mum will be very upset about it. Why Carmel?"

"It looks so peaceful. It's on a beach, and the weather will be great. I need to go somewhere alone where I can think, Becs. I can't focus right now on what I need to do. Not with work, Ben and the background noise of London. And even Jason, who was here again the other night."

"What did he want this time?"

"Oh, who knows? His wife has had the baby and he's just nervous. Why he thought he should come to me with that, I have no idea."

"So, what's bothering you the most?"

"Not having clarity about what to do. I've wanted to be a barrister my entire life, but now that it's in front of me as a real opportunity for the first time since I was with Jason, I can't seem to figure out the best way to make it happen."

"Tell me the options."

"Well, I believe there are three ways this might work. I'm trying to weigh each of them up against each other, but I can't decide what to do. The first and easiest option is moving back to Margate. I can quit my job and still afford to go back to university full time, which sounds great, but really isn't. The problem is that I'd need to be in London for classes a few times a week, and Margate is not the most convenient place to live for regular commuting to the city. And of course, I'd be living in the room I grew up in. But that aside, it's the fastest way to get to the end goal and will only take me one year."

"Next?"

"The second option is to take a flat, keep working full-time, and go to uni part time. This is also an easy option, assuming I can handle the class workload and my full time job, but it will take me twice as long to finish as option one."

"Third option?"

"That is going to the US if I get the scholarship. Which is highly unlikely, but still possible. But then, I don't know, I am not really keen on moving abroad and being all alone. And none of these options include Ben being in my life, except that if I stay in the country, I would be able to see him."

"I get it. When I lived in Paris for that year after uni, I could not wait to get home. I was lonely most of the time, even though I had friends and went out a lot. It just wasn't for me. You haven't heard from... which uni is it again?"

"The University of Texas."

"Right, well, when do you find out about that?"

"Not for another two weeks."

"A bit tight in terms of timing. What do you really want to do, Tamsin?"

"I have no idea."

"And how are things with Ben?"

"To be honest, I cooled it off a lot this week. It was getting a bit overwhelming, with the ball and the press. And then his ex-fiancée started to try to wiggle her way back into his life."

"Has he stopped that from happening?"

"Yes, but she really is something, Becs. For starters, she's a knockout. Just Google her now. Caroline Martin-Jessop."

"Oooh, I see what you mean."

"Yeah, so if he still has any feelings left for her, which he says he doesn't, I would be in real trouble."

"Agreed."

"I keep thinking that going to the US is my best option. But then, I ask myself how realistic is it to have a proper relationship with someone *thousands* of miles away? And the answer I come up with is *not realistic at all*. And even if I stay here, I won't have time for a relationship. I should just end it now, before it's too late."

"How do you *feel* about Ben?"

"Confused."

"Why don't you just see what happens between now and Christmas? Find out if you get the scholarship or not. The real question seems to be whether you want to keep seeing Ben and letting those feelings grow."

"I just don't know the answer to that right now."

"Well, as my mum always says to me, 'Pray on it', and she's not wrong."

"Your mum is always so upbeat and helpful. I love her."

"Who doesn't?"

"Thanks, Becca. I'm going with Ben to Tansley Hall on the fourteenth for their Christmas party, and I can't back out at this point, so I'll go with things as planned and see how I feel by then, before making any rash decisions. That will still give me time to get a new flat, or move home, or go abroad. We went to his friends' farm yesterday and stayed at the Hall and today we had a great time in Oxford, just doing touristy things."

"Is this Christmas party another fancy dinner event which requires a ball gown?"

"No. It's for the tenant farmers of Tansley Hall estate and Ben has said to wear whatever I like. Not very helpful, but his friend Suzie said most people will wear their Sunday best, so I'm sure I've got something suitable."

"Sounds like fun. I suggest you just go with things as you have them planned, at least for now. If you feel like you can't or don't want to be with Ben, then I'm sure you'll know it soon. What about his restaurant? What's happening with that?"

"Not much. He doesn't have a name for it yet, but I'm sure it's going to be very popular. How could it not be? He and his family know everyone. And Ben is a good cook. He's only made me breakfast so far, since I messed up our dinner plans the other night, but he's a creative chef."

They chatted about Becca's kids and her holiday plans, and said goodnight.

CHAPTER 56

Monday 2nd December

Sammy was so excited to see Tamsin when she came in to the office because he was bursting with news.

"The paperwork is all done on Shoreditch, Tamsin. They are ready to exchange this week."

"Great news, Sammy!"

Tamsin thought she should properly celebrate, since this was her first and second sale, concluding at the same time. Checking her phone, she saw that she had a message from Antony V, asking her again to come to his New Year's Eve party. Tamsin wouldn't be able to go now, but it was nice to be asked. She would be soaking up the sun in Carmel.

After work, Tamsin searched through her wardrobe for the right outfit for the Tansley Hall Christmas party. Ben called and she was about to tell him she just couldn't find anything to wear, when he sprang another surprise on her.

"Would you like to go to Monte Carlo for New Year's Eve, Tamsin?"

Monte Carlo? Where did he get these ideas?

"My old school chum Basil is having a party there on his yacht, and he's asked if I'd like to come, and invited you.

Since all of my friends know about you now, having seen us in the papers, I'm getting a lot of invitations. Although, I suspect most of them are so they can meet you."

"The thing is, Ben, I've booked a trip to Carmel, leaving on the twenty-ninth, and I won't be back until the second of January."

"Oh. I see. That sounds fun." His disappointment carried through the line and Tamsin felt bad, but she needed a break to sort things out in her mind.

"Are you ready for next Saturday's Christmas party?" he asked.

"I'm not sure. What type of clothes should I wear?"

"Whatever makes you feel comfortable. It's not formal. The kids will be wearing jeans and even my father will just have a wool or cashmere jumper on. The party is held in the Banquet Hall, but it's very low key."

"I'll figure it out. What should I bring?"

"Nothing. Just come as you are, but pack a bag to stay over."

Tamsin knew she'd have to order something for his dad and Pepper for Christmas.

What could they possibly need?

She had no idea.

After hanging up, she ordered a medium sized Christmas hamper from Fortnum and Mason for two hundred pounds, and hoped that would be the right gesture of thanks.

She found a pair of black Reiss trousers in her closet and paired them with her black cashmere jumper, thinking they looked good enough for the Christmas party.

A pair of new shoes might be a good idea, as she realized

her heels were looking tired. Not wanting to spend too much, but thinking that if she was going to, then doing so for an event like this made sense, she resolved to go to Manolo Blahnik and find a pair of heels to match. The shoes that went with the gown were too much bling.

CHAPTER 57

Tuesday 3rd December

After lunch, Tamsin returned to the office with a pair of heels in black leather, and felt she had what she needed for the Tansley Hall Christmas party. Her new Manolo's could double as work shoes, if she took care of them properly. That would make her feel less guilty buying them, considering how expensive they were.

It wasn't feeling very like Christmas yet, and there wasn't any snow in London, as usual, so Tamsin was keen to help put up a tree in the office and string it with lights.

Sammy and Lily had ordered a real tree and boxes of ornaments the week before, and they now put on 'Last Christmas' and broke out some Prosecco. Everyone helped and Tamsin was feeling much more in the Christmas mood as they all were after decorating the tree.

James had noticed that no one had asked him about having a Christmas party, and he hadn't booked anything. But now that things were looking up in the economy, he decided to surprise them, and hold a party after all. He asked Lily to find a venue for Friday night, only days away.

Lily was thrilled to be managing the booking and Sammy was giving her ideas about potential venues, although they both worried it would be hard to find any-where at such short notice.

"Tamsin, what do you think?" Sammy asked. "Should we go to Covent Garden, or somewhere around here?"

"I don't know. Somewhere we can have the best time, with a big enough bar, room for a DJ and dancing."

Tamsin was looking forward to the office party, although she was starting to run out of clothes for the events that seemed to be filling her diary lately.

"Maybe Antony V would come and help us out. What do you think?"

"I very much doubt that," said Tamsin. "He's not going to spend a precious Friday night in December being the DJ at an office Christmas party."

Feeling she deflated Sammy unnecessarily, she added, "But you could ask him. Why not?"

"Great. I'll do that and we'll keep looking for venues. Come on, Lily," Sammy said, while they went to get coffees for everyone.

"Tamsin?"

She could hear Ben's voice and turned around.

"Hi," he said as he appeared next to her. "Sorry, but there was no one at the front desk, so I thought I'd just walk over."

"Ben. Hi," she said, giving him a kiss. "What are you doing here?"

"I'm picking up some things from home, and then going back to Oxford, but was wondering if you would come with me to get some gifts for my father and Pepper."

"Sure," Tamsin said as she wheeled her chair around to see who else was in the office to take calls or walk-ins if she left.

"Give me a second," and she walked over to James's office to let him know she'd be leaving for a while.

"Viscount Tansley, is it?" he asked, looking over his glasses at her.

"Yes," she said, leaning half in his door, and rolling her eyes. "Just popping out for a gift for his father and step-mum."

"Ok. Ask him to come to the party, if you like."

"I thought it was employees only."

"Well, I feel generous this afternoon."

At that, she texted Sammy to let him know they'd need a bigger space as it was now a party of plus ones. He sent back a smiley face emoji and party streamers.

"Let's go," she said to Ben and they walked out onto Kings Road, where Ben had a car and driver waiting.

"What?" she asked when she saw the car. She was surprised to find they would be driven, rather than walk.

"Just faster this way. Hop in."

They were dropped off at Liberty.

"Pick something up for Pepper. Anything. More than one thing."

"Do gift cards count?"

"No."

"What brands does she like? What perfume does she wear?"

He hadn't any ideas, so Tamsin wandered around the cosmetics and accessories departments while Ben went to look for something for his father. Tamsin chose some items from Westman Atelier and Augustinus Bader and hoped Pepper would not think the brands were common, like she did champagne. Tamsin suggested they go somewhere else and buy matching cashmere sweaters for Pepper and Charles, and Ben agreed.

On the way, they passed Läderach chocolate and Tamsin insisted they get the milk chocolate with buttons, for themselves. After stopping a few more times for gifts, they were famished, and Ben asked her back to his place for dinner.

When they got there, dinner was already prepared, having been cooked by one of the chefs at Tansley Hall, who Tamsin found out followed Ben to whatever house he was staying at, to cook for him.

"I just thought it would be good to sit down and spend some time together," Ben said. "We've been running around like mad."

"Great idea," Tamsin said, as she sank into the sofa after dinner. Ben brought her some chocolate and a small glass of port. Eaten together, they tasted delicious.

"So," Ben said as he stroked her hair, "What's new with you, Tamsin?"

"I don't know. Oh yes, I do know. We are now having an office Christmas party on Friday night. Do you want to come?"

"Would you like me to?"

"Yes."

"Ok. Yes it is then. Will jeans do?"

"If you like."

"Right now, I would like to have some more chocolate," he said as he took the piece in her hand, broke it in two, and shared it with her, followed by a deep passionate kiss.

Tamsin took the lead this time and walked Ben to his bedroom. He followed, bringing more chocolate and champagne.

CHAPTER 58

Wednesday 4th December

When she woke in the morning, Tamsin remembered that she had promised to help Ben with the restaurant today. But she didn't have a change of clothes, and rush hour traffic made the relatively short distance to her place a long journey, whether by train or car.

She walked the five levels down to the kitchen, and found Ben having a coffee, and on the phone. Pouring herself a coffee, she regretted leaving her phone in the bedroom.

When he was done, Ben said, "Are you ready to help me out today, Tamsin? We're going to the architect's office and then to meet with the interior designer, Mina."

"I am. But once again, I am without a change of clothes."

"We need to fix that. Why don't you bring some of your things over and just leave them here? And also give me some to take to the Hall."

Worried about where this was going, but not wanting to make a fuss about it at this particular moment, Tamsin said, "Yes, good idea. But what about today? I really need to change."

Ben drove them to her flat and she made a short stop

before they visited the architect's office on Birchin Lane, to talk about how best to refurbish Cherwell and turn it into Ben's vision for the restaurant. Adding what she thought was little value to the conversation, she looked forward to the interior design decisions more eagerly, hoping she could contribute ideas about colours and surfaces.

A text came in from Sammy saying '*Sold!*' She knew she had to call him.

"Sold? Both flats?"

"Yes!" He could not contain himself, even though he would not be paid any commission for the flats, being new. "Congratulations, Tamsin."

"Thank you, Sammy. You were a big part of this and I hope James recognizes that. If Lavender Cottage and Cherwell exchange – that's what Ben is calling the building, by the way, Cherwell – then you will get paid for those, which is only right."

"Thanks, Tamsin. I've got to take Lily out for a drink after work to celebrate the sale of the flats. Can you come with us?"

"Not today. But I'll see you tomorrow. Have you two found a venue for the Christmas party yet?"

"YES. I've got The Ned booked for Friday night. It's so exciting!"

"Wow. I'm impressed, Sammy. How did you swing that?"

"They had a cancellation."

"And James is willing to pay for the entire evening, with drinks all around?"

"Yes."

"What about rooms? Can we all stay over? Or is he paying for cabs and Ubers?"

"Cabs and Ubers. There aren't any rooms left at The Ned on Friday anyway, unless of course you are a member."

"Well, I'm not. But maybe someone we work with is."

Maybe Ben is, she thought.

If so, they'd only have to take an elevator to get to bed, or whatever came after the party. She was still trying to treat Ben like a casual partner in her head, someone to only have fun with. And he was fun, but things were getting more serious, she could tell. She could *feel* it. And that wasn't the plan. Two more big parties, and then she'd be off to Margate and California and the whole thing with Ben would just fizzle out, she was sure.

"See you tomorrow, and thanks again, Sammy."

"Bye, Tamsin."

❄ ❄ ❄

"Ready?" Ben asked, as he was done with the architect and it was time to pick tiles, paint and cabinets.

"Yes."

"Who was that?"

"Sammy. The flats in Shoreditch have completed, so I've made my first two sales."

"Congratulations, Tamsin! I'm so happy for you," he said as they walked to the car. He gave her a huge hug and kiss. "This calls for a major celebration."

"Thanks, Ben. It's pretty exciting. I'll have to call my parents later and tell them."

"Can't you message them?"

"That's not really their thing, although they occasionally see my messages and reply. I call them every couple of days and let them know what's happening, so I'll do that tonight. In other news, the office Christmas party is going to be held at The Ned."

"Great. I have a membership there. Do we need a room?"

"Well, if you can get one, yes, please do. James is paying for cabs, but not rooms, and there aren't any available unless you have a membership."

"I'll sort it," said Ben.

CHAPTER 59

They drove to Marylebone and hurried from the car as they were running late for their appointment with the interior designer.

As they entered the studio, they saw Caroline was there, facing away from them. Tamsin was able to recognize her by her hair alone. It was so lustrous, full and blond.

"Hello, Caroline," said Ben.

"Ben." She turned around, smiled, and then looked Tamsin up and down, hiding a scowl. "This is Duke Alvarado," she said. He was the same man she had been all over at the ball.

Carlos and Ben shook hands and Ben introduced Tamsin.

"What are you doing here, Ben? Your house doesn't need any changes," Caroline said.

Tamsin thought that was a dig, knowing Caroline had been there only the other day.

"I'm here for my new restaurant."

"Finally opening one of your own?"

It was obvious to Tamsin that Caroline already knew this to be true, and just wanted to irritate Ben further.

"Yes. We need to go. Excuse us," Ben said as he waved at Mina, the designer who was waiting for them. He took Tamsin's hand and they walked to the back of the showroom.

After considering many different colours and textures, Ben tentatively chose several products for the restaurant, including tables and chairs, floor and wall tiles and the kitchen counters. Tamsin hoped that all of the orders could be cancelled if the building purchase did not go through. The total came to four hundred thousand pounds, some of which was due immediately. Tamsin had never seen anything like the spending Ben had just done. He waved a card like magic, and things were paid for.

They left the design studio and went back to Kensington. After their long day, Tamsin thought a glass of wine was in order, and possibly some food.

"I know I still have not made you dinner, but given all the festivities lately – and those yet to come – I hope you don't mind waiting a little bit longer, for a day when I can organize a meal properly," said Ben, having suggested they go back to his house and order in.

"So for tonight's dinner, Chinese?" he asked as he waved a menu at her.

Tamsin laughed.

"Perfectly happy with that."

After dinner, Tamsin asked Ben what the rooms at The Ned were like and if he had managed to get one.

"Not yet. I'll do it now."

CHAPTER 60

Office Christmas Party – Friday 6th December

Tamsin pulled her cashmere sweater out of her wardrobe, only to find that the moths had been at it, and it could not be worn. There was a large hole in the middle of one arm.

She'd have to find something else, and fast, since the office party was starting in two hours. Everyone had left the office at noon, and she hadn't bothered checking her clothes until now.

What were the odds the sweater would be lunch for a moth?

She had only worn it a few weeks before.

The new heels she had bought were amazing, and she'd been wearing them each day when she got home, so she wouldn't get blisters tonight.

As she looked further in her cupboard, she found a mini skirt she liked and a pair of tights with crystals. Normally naff, but not at Christmas.

Now all she needed was a jumper or a blouse. A red silk top she rarely wore was hidden in the back of her wardrobe, and she hoped it would not be too crumpled. She had decided to get rid of it, but hadn't done so yet. It worked.

Ben was picking her up at six and they were having

dinner at The Ned first, before the party. Being his girl-friend, if that's what she was, definitely had some major benefits. Like getting a room when the hotel was full, and other surprises.

As she looked in the mirror, Tamsin felt ready for tonight and was excited about the party. In fact, her mood had been very good for several weeks, even though she was a bit stressed out and conflicted about what to do about uni and her living arrangements.

Could it be Ben who was causing this marked improvement in her mood? Maybe it was that, and confronting Jason, which had given her a sense of freedom. Or was she feeling good about something else?

Selling the cottage and flats had helped. Being independent was very important to Tamsin. Perhaps more important to her than she had known before, and it was a wonderful feeling to be making her own way, while also having a very attentive and attractive man by her side. She was thrilled to have enough money now to get her own flat and have choices, even if she didn't know what she wanted to do yet.

The buzzer for her flat rang. It was Ben.

"Can you come down, or should I come up?" he asked.

She hadn't let Ben in to see the flat yet and didn't want to show it to him now. It would be strange having another man in the place she had shared with Jason for so long.

"I'll be right down."

She put on her lipstick, checked her hair one more time, and closed the door behind her.

When they got to The Ned, they checked into their room, and had dinner. They'd decided to eat at Kaia and took their time, since it was still early.

"Have you heard back from the University of Texas yet?" Ben asked.

"Not yet. But the admission letters can be mailed out as late as December fifteenth, so I might not find out for a while yet. I hope they also send the answer by email."

"Are you excited about the prospect of attending university in Texas?"

Tamsin wasn't sure excited was the word, but she was anxious to know if she had been accepted. It would solve a lot of problems having a full scholarship, but create new choices and challenges.

She'd been learning about how to reduce anxiety in a self-help book she was reading, and the advice was to focus on what she could control. Right now, that was how she'd handle this evening, by not worrying about the future.

"I am, but I'm letting myself not think about it until the answer comes through."

"That seems sensible. What are you planning to get up to in Carmel?"

"I haven't really sorted that out yet. I've booked one restaurant, but other than that, I just plan on taking long walks on the beach, and relaxing, while I think everything through. By the time I go home for Christmas, I'll know whether going to Texas is an option, or not. And if it isn't, then I need to decide if I will stay at my parents or get my own flat. I have to move out before Christmas."

"Would you like me to help you with that? I can organize a mover for you."

"I don't have any furniture of my own, just clothes and personal things, so I was going to ask Andrew and Nico to help me on the twenty-first. Nico's parents own a fleet of delivery vans, and he said he could borrow one and do the driving."

"Let me know if you change your mind."

"I will."

After dinner they went to their room and Tamsin flopped on the bed while Ben went back downstairs to meet a friend, who was also a member of the private club, for a quick drink. Tamsin was really tired, but feeling good.

Antony V had said he would DJ the party for them, but outside entertainment was not allowed. Shame, Tamsin thought, as she wanted to hear what he played. Since she had told him she was going to be in California for New Year's Eve, he finally stopped asking her to come to his New Year's party but had insisted that she go up to Liverpool in January for his next party.

From what she could tell, he did about ten parties a year and made a very good living doing it. She'd rather go to the one he was having in Ibiza in February, but she accepted his invitation for Liverpool.

When Ben returned, they changed their clothes and went downstairs to join the party, which had been going for a couple of hours already.

CHAPTER 61

"Tamsin!" said James as she walked in. He had obviously been drinking for a while, and he leaned in to Tamsin and said, "How's it going, Tamsin? He's a Viscount. Are you aware of that?"

"Yes, James. I'm aware," she said as she gently pushed his arm to help him straighten up. He was pissed. "Do you have a room here tonight, James?"

"Yes. My wife is upstairs now. She's coming down later."

Good, thought Tamsin.

She waved Lily over and asked her to keep an eye out for Morwenna, James's wife. She hoped James would get up to his room as soon as possible, since he was in no state to be talking to people.

The banquet room was dark and the music was booming through the speakers. Sammy had bought glow in the dark necklaces and everyone was wearing them.

It was definitely a party for drinking, Tamsin thought, and she was not really in the mood for that tonight. Needing a break, she left Ben and a colleague talking and went to get some air.

As she entered the main corridor, she saw Caroline

and her Duke snogging in the hall. She started to turn the other way, but Caroline had seen her.

"Tamsin. How bizarre to run into you again. What you are you doing here?"

"We're at my office Christmas party."

"We?"

Tamsin was sure Caroline knew she was here with Ben.

"Yes. Ben's in there," she nodded to the room adjacent.

At that moment, Ben came out and said, "Oh, there you are. I was looking for you."

"Ben," said Caroline.

At the sound of her voice, his whole body stiffened.

"What are you doing here, Caroline?" he asked.

"Carlos and I are having dinner with friends. Are you going to the Shard on New Year's?"

"No," Ben said, although that had been his plan. "Goodnight, Caroline," Ben added and he and Tamsin went back to the party.

Once they had left Caroline behind, he said, "If Caroline is going to the Shard for New Year's Eve, I think I'll have to give it a miss. Since you're going to be in California, I'll go to Monte Carlo instead."

❄ ❄ ❄

"Sir, I mean Lord. Tamsin is amazing," slurred Sammy as he put his arm around Ben and tried to hug Tamsin at the same time.

Too much alcohol already, thought Tamsin.

"Yes, she certainly is amazing," said Ben, trying to help Sammy stay upright.

Tamsin turned to Lily and mouthed 'Cab?' Lily nodded and said she was working on it. Trying to find a taxi on a Friday night in December in central London was near impossible, Uber or otherwise.

After bundling Sammy and Lily into a cab thirty minutes later, and helping Morwenna get James to his hotel room, Tamsin and Ben decided to call it a night.

Not having had too much to drink themselves, but wired from the festivities, running into Caroline and the general gaiety of the Christmas party, Ben opened a bottle of champagne that he had ordered to be there when they got back to their suite.

It was wonderful to have a responsible man in her life who was attentive to her needs, Tamsin thought. And Ben was attentive in more ways than one. They drank more champagne and he asked her, as they lay in bed and he stroked her cheek, "Do you have to go to Carmel, Tamsin? Can you come to Monte Carlo with me instead?"

She almost said yes, but held her ground.

"Well, I could, Ben. But I really need to clear my head," she said, as she stroked his arm and kissed him, trying to make him lose interest in talking.

It worked and he responded to her touch. They turned out the light.

❄ ❄ ❄

When Tamsin woke, Ben was not there. She was glad, because she was getting more confused about her feelings for Ben every time they spent a night together. If the only way to stop the confusion was to quit seeing Ben, then that's what she would do. But she could not deny that she was really enjoying spending time with him.

She showered and dressed and Ben returned looking like a Cheshire cat, the grin on his face was so wide.

"Let's go get some breakfast, beautiful," he said.

After they ate, Ben had his driver drop her off before he headed back to Oxford, and she spent the rest of the day figuring out what to give to charity and what was left to pack for her move. She'd promised Jason the flat back by Christmas, so time was running out.

CHAPTER 62

Monday 9th December

On Monday, Ben's building purchase was moving along and it was starting to look like he might get the keys before the end of the year. That was a relief to Tamsin, since she didn't think Ben had enough time to get a new restaurant open by Easter if the sale did not complete this year. He still hadn't landed on a name for it. She liked his father's idea, *Tansley's*. It sounded great to her.

Tamsin was unsure about what to wear to the Christmas party at Tansley Hall on Saturday, and had not bought Ben a gift yet.

She called Andrew first for help with what to wear, and then called Nico, to share her ideas about what to get for Ben and ask his opinion.

"Do you have any sexy jeans?" Andrew asked.

"No."

"What about trousers?"

"Sexy trousers? No. I haven't got anything that looks great. All my clothes are just so boring. I want a nice, comfortable top, if nothing else. Where can I find one?"

"Let's go shopping together after work today," said Andrew.

After checking about ten different shops, they finally decided on a white cotton jumper with crystals from Club Monaco in Sloane Square, and went for a drink afterwards.

"What are you going to do about moving?" Andrew asked.

"I haven't got a clue. I don't have much stuff. Could you help me move it to my parents, if it comes to that? Nico said he will drive the van."

"If it comes to that. But let's hope it doesn't. How are things with Lord Tansley?"

"Good." Tamsin didn't want to elaborate, but she was increasingly torn about whether to keep seeing Ben or not. If she was moving abroad, continuing to see him was going to make that harder for both of them.

They went to Crazy Pizza for dinner, which was always so much fun, and then Tamsin took the tube home, wondering when she would hear from the University of Texas.

CHAPTER 63

Tuesday 10th December

Tamsin was deep in thought, reviewing a contract for Ben's restaurant, when her phone pinged. It was an email from the University of Texas saying that her application had been approved. There were several attachments and a welcome pack with all the things she needed to know, including where her room would be on campus.

She closed it and put her phone aside so she could concentrate. But her mind kept going back to the email.

She decided to go out and get a gift for Ben, before the Tansley Hall Christmas party. Or at least she'd start looking for something. Nico hadn't been around when she had called the other day, so she tried him again while she got ready to leave the office.

"Help, Nico. I have no idea what to buy Ben for Christmas. Do you have any ideas?" was the voice note she left for him.

He pinged back some ideas, saying he was working and couldn't talk until later. Cashmere sweater. Cufflinks. Cologne. All good ideas, but oh so boring. She wanted to strike the right balance between saying 'I like you' and 'Let's get married'.

A gift that would say, 'I like you enough to have bought

you a gift that took some effort to think of' but that didn't convey love, since, after all, it wasn't love she felt for Ben.

Was it? She wasn't sure anymore.

After checking a few shops at lunch, she gave up on Christmas shopping for Ben, having bought some things for her mum, dad and Becca instead, and went back to the office.

CHAPTER 64

Wednesday 11th December

When Tamsin walked into the office, Sammy told her that the legal contracts for Lavender Cottage were ready for exchange, and Ben called to ask Tamsin when he could get the keys. The seventeenth was the first date that would be possible, six days from now, and when they spoke again, he asked her to come up to Oxford by train the day after he got the keys. He would make dinner, and she could stay over, if she liked.

"But, will the cottage be ready by then to stay in?" she asked. "It will need a good clean, for one thing. One day isn't a lot of time to get that sorted."

"Not a problem at all. I will have it ready for you for dinner on the eighteenth and I hope you will stay the night and help me with Cherwell if there is anything else left to be done next week to complete the purchase."

She agreed and stepped out to buy a few things to wear for Christmas. While waiting at a traffic light, she heard a voice she recognized calling out behind her.

"Tamsin?"

She turned around.

"Jason. How are you?"

"I'm good. I'm really good. I'm taking some time off work to spend with Amber and the baby. Thank you so much for letting me in that night and just sitting with me."

"You are welcome. What are you doing around here?"

"Just buying something for the baby and Amber for Christmas."

"That's nice. What did you have? A boy or a girl?"

"We had a boy. He's called Nathan, after my dad."

"Congratulations again, Jason."

He nodded and smiled.

"I was thinking, if you want to stay to the end of the year, don't feel you need to be out of the flat by Christmas. I really do need to sell it, but I realized how unfair it was to ask you to leave just before Christmas."

It had been unfair, but Tamsin knew her energy was better spent on other things, rather than brooding over the past. So she said,

"Thanks, Jason, but that probably won't be necessary. I'll be down in Margate with my parents from the twenty-third, so I expect you can go in any time after that and maybe earlier. I'll push the keys through the letter box when I lock up."

"Ok, well, it's really nice to see you, Tamsin, and I know I said it that night, but I didn't say it enough. I am truly sorry for how I treated you. You deserve much better than me."

"All is forgiven, Jason," she said, and she meant it. The animosity of the last two years was gone now.

CHAPTER 65

Back at her office, she looked at the listings for some of the other properties that had come in recently to be sold, and considered which ones she could start advertising after Christmas. Then she remembered that she had a decision to make – one of many – and called Becca.

"Can you talk?" she asked.

"Not right now. But how about tonight? Do you want to drop by?"

Tamsin considered it but said no, she'd call Becca when she got home, rather than drop by her house. With the kids and Chris and the nanny there, it would be hard for Becca and Tamsin to talk properly. She would go home, have a glass of wine and try to sort out her thoughts about Texas, before calling Becca.

When she got home, she made a list of the pros and cons of attending uni in Austin – one of many such lists she had made over the last two days. It was obvious. The answer was that she should go to the US, give up the flat, and not look back. But that scenario meant things would be over with Ben. And for some reason, that really mattered to her now.

She could not wait for the trip to Carmel. But first, she

had to attend the Tansley Hall Christmas party and was really looking forward to it.

Talking to Becca did not help her sort out her thoughts any further, which was unusual, so she decided to keep going through her clothes and kitchen cupboards, being ruthless about what to keep and what to give away and finally landed on what to get Ben for Christmas.

CHAPTER 66

Saturday 14th December

Tamsin had two bags with her, one to be left at Ben's house in Kensington, and one for her trip to Tansley Hall for the Christmas party. She also had a garment bag, in which she had packed the ball gown, just in case it was called for while she was in Oxford. Ben put everything in the boot and then they got on the motorway.

In one overnight bag was Ben's Christmas gift, and Tamsin hoped he liked it. She had landed on a Farer watch. Not the most expensive one they had, but a really good looking one she was sure he would like.

The long winding driveway to the Hall was now lined with snow and the front entrance sparkled with small, tastefully selected and placed white lights.

Helen greeted her and Tamsin's bags were taken to the Marlowe Suite.

In the hall foyer was the largest Christmas tree Tamsin had ever seen. It was decorated with coloured lights, which was Tamsin's favourite way to dress a tree.

The Hall smelled of cinnamon and cloves and a mince pie was offered to her, along with English sparkling wine. At first she thought it was champagne, but Ben saw the look of surprise on her face and shook his head, so she figured out what it was.

The main living room had a roaring fire, and Tamsin and Ben were left on their own to settle in and relax after their long journey. The roads had all been very busy and the trip took twice as long on the M40 as they had expected. Everyone seemed to be gearing up for Christmas.

Pepper joined them, followed by Lady Philippa and they all toasted each other with a glass of the English sparkling wine.

"This is very nice," said Tamsin, after taking a sip.

"Thank you," said Pepper. "Has Ben told you about our vineyard, Tamsin?"

She looked at him, since this was news to her.

"No. I wasn't aware you had one."

"Yes. We produce this award-winning wine."

Since the bottle was labelled 'Guysborough', Tamsin would not have guessed it had anything to do with the Smythe-Jones family, or Tansley Hall. But Ben said that it was Pepper's surname.

"It's really delicious," Tamsin said as she took a second glass. For some reason, Pepper still made her nervous and she kept forgetting to ask Ben if that was her given name or a nickname.

"Well, Tamsin, it looks like the cottage will be Harry's this week," said Lady Philippa.

"Yes, I'm very happy for you both."

"Now if only the building purchase could move along at the same speed."

"Gran, it's not Tamsin's fault that has stalled."

"I wouldn't dream of suggesting such a thing, Harry,

and only mention it in case Tamsin can do anything about it. Can you, Tamsin?"

Tamsin nearly choked on her mince pie. Of course there was nothing she could do to speed up the purchase. It was all with the lawyers and any delay was up to them to resolve.

She had been worried that mixing business and pleasure would get murky and now it was.

Her instinct had been not to attend the Tansley Hall Christmas party and she hoped she would not be grilled further. What would Ben's father Charles say when he arrived? Tamsin was struggling to keep calm, and excused herself before the anxiety she felt took hold of her.

She placed her hands under the cold running water of the tap to lower her temperature. Sometimes this helped when she got stressed in a situation she could not get out of. There was a knock on the bathroom door.

"Tamsin," Ben whispered. "Are you ok?"

"Yes, yes. Fine, Ben." She wiped tears from her eyes. "I'll be right out."

Tamsin felt silly. She didn't care if Ben's grandmother asked her questions she couldn't answer. It was being put on the spot that had made her anxious and feel the need to get away.

But Tamsin knew that even when people didn't mean to make her nervous, which set off anxiety responses of sweating palms and getting hot, they often did. She sat down on the dressing room table chair and Helen came in. She had brought Tamsin's make-up bag, having unpacked her carryall upstairs.

"Thank you, Helen," she said as she re-applied her

concealer and some powder. She followed Helen to her suite and found Ben waiting for her there. He walked over and gave her a hug and a kiss on the forehead.

Taking her hands, he said, "I'm sorry about Gran. I told her that once we agreed a price, you would not be responsible for moving the sale along and if anyone is to blame, it's me, for not chasing our lawyers. But never mind all of that. Are you alright?"

"Yes. I have problems with anxiety sometimes, and when I feel overwhelmed, I just need to get out of whatever situation I am in and take a breath."

"Okay," he said as he stroked her hair. "Can I give you your Christmas present now? I know you will be with your parents on the day, and I'm very excited about the gift I have for you."

Tamsin changed into something more relaxing and sat cross legged on the sofa. The suite had a bedroom, sitting room and large dressing room with an en suite washroom, and she wanted to relax before the party.

"That sounds great," she said, as she reached over to a bowl of mint chocolate wafers and took two. "Let me get yours as well," she said, but Ben said that could wait and she should open hers first. He handed her a beautifully wrapped box, with multiple ribbons and bows.

"I hope you like it, but if you don't, we can return it."

"I'm sure I will!" she said. As she unwrapped the Christmas paper, she could see a powder pink box and written on it was Boodles. A fine English jewellery firm, with several boutiques that Tamsin had walked by, but never gone into. Inside was a jewel box and when she opened the lid, she found a pair of diamond earrings. They were exquisite.

"Ben! This is far too much!" she said.

"Nonsense." He came to sit closer to her and she reached out to hug and kiss him.

"Thank you so much."

"Do you like them?"

"I LOVE them. I will never take them off, they are so beautiful."

She tried the diamond stud earrings on, and they looked even better than they did in the box.

"What are you wearing to the party later?" Ben asked.

"Jeans. I honestly could not decide what to wear, so I bought a really pretty top and a new pair of jeans." She got up to show the new jumper to Ben.

"That will be perfect. I'll wear jeans as well. Dinner is in the Marchand Room, which can be draughty, but the fires will be roaring. The earrings will look great with that. Shall we get ready to go downstairs and join everyone else? If Gideon is here, you can finally meet him."

"Ok, but first, I have something for you as well."

She got up to retrieve a box from her bag, which Helen had placed in the dressing room.

"This is for you," she said as she handed him the gift. "Merry Christmas, Ben."

As he unwrapped the box, he said, "Oh wow, Tamsin. This is great. I have been meaning to buy one of these."

"Really?"

"Honestly. I just couldn't decide which type and which colour, since there are so many great options."

"I know. I saw this one a while ago and thought it would suit you."

"It does. Thank you very much."

He leaned over to kiss her on the lips, and held her chin for just a moment, looked in her eyes, and then gave her a hug, while he placed the watch on his wrist.

"Chocolate?" she asked.

"Better not. We are going to eat a lot later," he said. "I'm saving my appetite for all the puddings. Let's go downstairs and see who else has arrived."

Tamsin changed her clothes and met Ben in the hallway.

"Giles!" Ben said when they entered the main drawing room. They embraced and Giles gave Tamsin a kiss on the cheek.

"You look great, Tamsin."

"Thank you, Giles."

"Have you been able to help Ben pick a name for the restaurant, Tamsin?"

"No, I haven't been working on that, but my honest view is that Tansley's is the best name."

"I agree!" said Giles.

"I'm still thinking about it," said Ben.

After a short while, Gideon entered the room and Ben introduced his elusive friend to Tamsin.

"Hello, Gideon. It's nice to meet you."

"Likewise. I'm so glad you found a place for Ben to live, Tamsin. Really enjoyed having Ben around, but I'm a writer, and I need my space."

"Ha-ha, Gideon," said Ben. "He's not just a writer, Tamsin. This is Gideon Guyde, the famous food writer."

She had never heard of him, but said, "That's great. Do you write books or articles...?"

They talked for a while as the room started to fill up.

Then Ben left Tamsin to greet some guests with his father and Pepper.

By seven-thirty, the ballroom was full and people were starting to take their places for dinner. The dining tables were laid out in a large U shape, and there were over two hundred guests.

Dinner was more extravagant than the night Tamsin had been here the first time, and she remembered the tips Ben had given her about how to indicate to the servers that she had enough food and drink.

Dancing would be held in the adjacent room and Tamsin wondered if people would stay and what type of music would be played.

At nine-thirty, everyone was dancing, or had left for the evening. The music varied and there were many local musicians, singing and playing various instruments, including several people who lived on the Tansley estate. There was also a choir, which led them all in Christmas carols and hymns.

The dessert table was set and people were helping themselves to puddings and biscuits, the children running and hiding, and loading up on sugar.

At eleven o'clock, Tamsin was ready to sleep. She said goodnight, gave Ben a kiss, and went to her suite. Ben had to mingle further with the tenants of the estate and Tamsin wanted to have a bath and look more closely at her new diamond earrings.

CHAPTER 67

Wednesday 18th December

The completion on Lavender Cottage went through as expected on the seventeenth, and on the eighteenth, Tamsin took the train to Oxford and Ben picked her up at the station. Since she had given him an overnight bag on the weekend, she didn't need to bring clothes with her this time.

As they drove towards Lavender Cottage, Tamsin could not believe the transformation that had occurred at the cottage in just one day, since Ben had gotten the keys.

The exterior of the house had been painted, and the garden had been completely cleared of all leaves and was now extremely tidy. The front door had a Christmas wreath, and the windows were framed with Christmas lights.

Inside, the house was filled with the smell of pine and spruce. Ben had brought in a florist to make and place garlands on the fireplace and along the staircase and create a beautiful centrepiece for the dining table. He'd also filled the house with the most perfect furniture for a country cottage and Tamsin was impressed.

"So," he asked her with anticipation as they stepped inside, "Do you like it?"

"Like it? It's a completely different house! I LOVE it."

"I'm not finished, of course," he said. "But not bad for one day, I think."

"Agreed. It looks perfect, Ben," she said and reached up to kiss him.

He took her things upstairs and she followed, finding a new pair of pink silk pyjamas, a soft cosy robe, slippers and toiletries on the bed.

"Just in case you didn't pack those," he said.

It was likely an idea from Helen, Tamsin thought, since Tansley Hall was fully equipped at all times for every guest and their needs. It was one of the first things she remembered about her unexpected stay there. Just having a new toothbrush available for her had put her at ease, not to mention the silk eye mask and everything else they pampered their guests with.

She was so thrilled that Ben had a place of his own in Oxford now. And selfishly, she thought it would be much better for them as well.

Today she had to tell Ben about Texas, and she was not sure how or even what she was going to say.

Ben had the entire evening planned out. First, they would dress the Christmas tree, while having hot chocolate. Then, they would have dinner. After that, they would take a walk around his new neighbourhood to see how others had decorated their houses and get ideas for next year.

Somehow, she'd have to squeeze in the news about studying law and her plans.

Andrew and Nico were going to help her move her

things on the twenty-first from Hammersmith to her parent's house in Margate.

She was all ready for her trip to Carmel on the twenty-ninth, but the bits in between, like where she was going to attend uni and where she was going to live, were still up in the air.

Ben had selected a lovely tree, which he stood by the fireplace, and they dressed it with lights and ornaments and enjoyed hot chocolate together.

Dinner was chicken Kiev and mashed potatoes, a dish that Tamsin really liked. They clinked glasses and ate more than they should have, since Ben had made too much food.

Now she *knew* he was a fabulous cook.

They put the small amount of leftovers in the composter in the yard, and went for a walk in the brisk evening air. The houses near Ben's were all very lovely, and Tamsin hoped he would be happy here. Others were out for an evening stroll and said hello as they passed each other. She was having a wonderful time and dreaded having to tell Ben about her plans.

When they got back to the cottage, Tamsin resigned herself to telling Ben about being accepted to university in the US.

❄ ❄ ❄

"I see," he said, after she shared the news. "So, when are you leaving for Texas?"

"January fifth."

"And everything there is sorted out? How will you get around?"

"Yes, it's all fine. I'll be living on campus, so I won't need a car, but if I do, I'll get one."

"Well, I'm really happy for you, Tamsin. If this is what you want to do, I could not be happier for you," he said.

But he looked and sounded miserable, thought Tamsin, even though he was trying very hard to hide it.

"Yes, I mean, I can't really say no, can I? All expenses are paid, except my flight to Texas. Which reminds me, I need to book that as soon as possible."

"So, let's enjoy our evening," he said as he reached out his hand for her and pulled her in close to him on the sofa.

"Yes, let's do that."

❄ ❄ ❄

Ben dropped Tamsin at the train station the next morning and wished her the best with her move.

They didn't have any plans to see each other before she left for Texas.

Ben said there was a chance he would be in London the next day, and if so, he would like to see Tamsin, before she left the UK.

The countertop sample for the restaurant was due to arrive at the design showroom in Marylebone, and Ben would need to see it and put the order in before Christmas in order for the counter to arrive from Italy by March. It was a pivotal part of the opening schedule and he was counting on it being done on time.

Tamsin felt very down on the train ride home and her malaise continued throughout her moving day.

CHAPTER 68

Saturday 21st December

Ben hadn't been able to make it on Friday, and Tamsin had been disappointed. The move had gone smoothly, and she was glad to be out of the flat she'd shared with Jason.

Her friends had been brilliant helping Tamsin move, and to thank them, she'd taken them out for fish and chips. She and Nico and Andrew enjoyed a walk on the beach before they headed back to London.

Tamsin's mum was thrilled to see her and her father was quiet, as he always was, but she could tell he was very excited to have her home.

She sat down with them in the evening and explained the plans she had. She would be going to Carmel for a few nights and then leaving for Texas.

No matter how many times she relayed her plans, or ran through them in her head, she just wasn't excited about going to America.

Unless she changed her mind while she was in Carmel, she was going to Texas, and would be leaving Margate, her parents, Ben, and her life behind.

CHAPTER 69

Christmas Eve

On Christmas Eve, the hotel Tamsin had booked in Carmel called with bad news. There had been a flood at the hotel earlier in the day and they'd had to close the entire hotel for the remainder of the year.

They had been able to organize different hotels for Tamsin to stay in, but it meant she would spend her holiday changing hotels every night.

And they had so far been unable to secure anywhere for her to stay on New Year's Eve, although they were looking into that.

Deciding this was too much disruption to a short holiday, Tamsin decided to take the refund they offered instead.

Extremely disappointed, she tried to be upbeat for her parents' party that evening, but was really feeling low. Ben called and she told him the bad news. He seemed elated.

"A-ha! Well then, Tamsin, how would you like to go with me to Monte Carlo for New Year's Eve after all?"

"I don't know, Ben. It's my birthday too, and I..."

"Your birthday?! Is on New Year's Eve?! But you never said."

"I know. I don't like to make a big deal out of it."

"Think about it. Please. I've booked a sea view suite at the Hotel Hermitage. We'd need to spend some time on Basil's yacht for the party that evening, but if you fly out with me on the twenty-ninth, we can have three nights together before you have to leave for Texas."

Tamsin knew it was a bad idea.

Spending three nights with Ben in Monte Carlo would surely cause her to re-think her plans.

Yet she was sure about going to Texas.

Wasn't she?

"That's really nice of you to invite me, Ben. I will think about it, ok?" She wanted to just hide in her room, but her parents were calling her downstairs to see their guests. "I have to go and will let you know soon."

CHAPTER 70

Christmas Day

Feeling refreshed, Tamsin woke up on Christmas Day having decided to go with Ben to Monte Carlo.

"Mum, dad, I've decided to go to Monte Carlo with Ben and ring in the New Year there with him," she said as they had breakfast.

"That sounds exciting, dear. We're so sorry your trip to Carmel has been cancelled, but going to Monte Carlo will be fun. Will Ben come and pick you up, and we can finally meet him?" her mother asked.

"No. Ben is in Oxford, so he will be sending a car to pick me up from here and take me to his house in London, and then we'll take his family plane to Monaco."

"Are you planning to continue seeing Ben when you are away in Texas, Tamsin?" asked her father.

"No, dad. I am going to have to tell him before New Year's that a long-distance relationship is not going to work out. I'm going to be very busy with my studies, and he has a restaurant to get off the ground by Easter."

"I see."

"Do you think it's somehow possible we could make it work, being that far apart?" she asked her father.

"Not forever, but maybe for the short time you need to be away for university. If you are right for each other."

Tamsin kept replaying what her father had said, '*If you are right for each other.*'

Were they right for each other?

Maybe they were. But no matter which way she looked at it, she didn't see how things could work out with Ben. They were just too different, for a start. He was going to be an Earl someday and she could barely tell the difference between the knives to use for dinner at his house, never mind how to talk to aristocrats when Ben was not around.

And she was certain that distance would crush the feelings they had, because although they could do video calls every day if they had time, it just wasn't the same as being together in the same place. He would get tired of her, and she would get tired of having to try so hard to stay connected.

But the thought that maybe it could work, if they were right for each other, swirled around and kept her awake most of the night.

CHAPTER 71

Monte Carlo – Sunday 29th December

On the twenty-ninth, a chauffeur arrived to take Tamsin from her parent's house to the private plane at Heathrow where she and Ben would fly to Monte Carlo. Since she had never been to Monte Carlo, she had no idea what to wear. She was sure that nothing she owned would be suitable, so she wore jeans and a jumper, a leather jacket, and packed more clothes than she needed. This included the white jumper she had worn to the Christmas party at Tansley Hall, her red one-shoulder dress, her blue gown from the ball and her new black heels. None of it seemed suitable, but they were the best options she had.

Tamsin admired the beauty of the plane when they got on board. She had never been on a private jet before. It was much larger than she thought it would be and very comfortable. Other than Tamsin and Ben, there were no other guests, just two stewards and two pilots. The plane belonged to Ben's father, Charles, and was used for private travel by Ben on occasion.

"Wow! Ben. This is really something," said Tamsin as she ran her hand along the leather seat, which was similar in texture to the seat in the Bentley. Supple, soft and welcoming.

"I guess I don't think about it much," Ben said. "But yes, private air travel can be very nice."

It was clear to Tamsin that Ben's previous girlfriends came from families with their own planes as well. He had never dated someone from a background like Tamsin's, and she had never dated anyone who was as wealthy as Ben and his family. It did take getting used to.

They were offered lunch, of salmon and samphire, small potatoes and capers, and Tamsin took in the spectacular view as they landed. Monte Carlo looked crowded and compact, but beautiful.

When they arrived at the hotel, they checked into their suite, which had a sea view, like Ben had said, and a stunning terrace. Although it wasn't warm outside, it was much warmer than London. They had some coffee on their large balcony, and planned their evenings, before taking a walk at the harbour.

Ben had secretly bought the other two gowns Tamsin had tried on at Civello and he'd packed and brought them as a surprise for Tamsin. All three gowns were neatly laid out on the bed with the matching shoes, bags and gloves when they returned to the room. Herve, the hotel stylist, had organized for the hotel's top hair consultant to style Ben and Tamsin's hair each evening before going out and for someone to do Tamsin's make-up.

This evening, they would have dinner in a private dining room at the hotel, with other key guests, including some foreign dignitaries and two members of European

Royal families. Tamsin chose the emerald green dress to wear.

Tomorrow, they agreed they would do something more casual, for which her red dress would suffice, and on the thirty-first, they would have dinner in their suite, with views of the harbour, before going to Basil's party on his yacht. For that, Tamsin would wear the turquoise gown and remove the detachable crinoline. She could hardly wait to wear that incredible gown.

CHAPTER 72

New Year's Eve

Tamsin was having a fantastic time and was sad this was the last night she would spend with Ben before she moved to Texas.

The trip to Monte Carlo had been so much more fun than she could have imagined it would be, and she no longer regretted not going to Carmel.

Each day had been perfect, with warm weather, and today, her birthday, had been extra special.

Ben had booked a private suite for them at the spa as a birthday gift to Tamsin. They both had a massage and a facial and were served the Guysborough English sparkling wine afterwards, which Tamsin thought was a very sweet gesture. Ben had brought a case with him on the plane and given our bottles to the staff as gifts. He and his family had been regular guests at the hotel since it had opened over a hundred years ago.

Dinner each evening had been delicious and they had both met some interesting people on this trip from all over the world.

As they got ready to go to Basil's yacht in the harbour, Tamsin went outside onto the balcony to get some air. The last three days with Ben had been magical, and she was thrilled to be having this adventure with him.

Ben came out and wrapped his arms around Tamsin. She turned around and put her arms around his neck, lightly kissing him.

"Thank you for inviting me to Monte Carlo, Ben. I've had the best time ever."

"Have you enjoyed your birthday, Tamsin?"

"Yes, and I'm looking forward to ringing in the new year with you for the first time."

At that, Ben pulled something out of his jacket pocket. It was a small jewel box. He opened it and inside was the biggest diamond ring Tamsin had ever seen.

"Will you marry me, Tamsin?" Ben asked.

"Of course I will," she said as he placed the ring on her hand, and they kissed under the moonlight on the balcony.

"This calls for champagne," said Ben.

"Agreed," said Tamsin, as Ben walked from the balcony into their suite at the Hotel Hermitage to retrieve it.

"Let me come with you," Tamsin said, assuming he had to call down to reception to order it, and, getting chilly in the night air, she preferred to wait inside.

"No need," he said, and was back with two champagne flutes and a bottle in no time. "Here you are, beautiful," Ben said and he handed Tamsin a glass, clinking his with hers.

"But, when...?"

"I ordered it earlier, in the hope that you would accept my proposal of marriage."

"Cheeky," Tamsin said, but happy Ben was confident she would say yes.

As she took a sip, she said, "This is *delicious*, Ben. What brand is it?"

"Well, good story. It's a non-alcoholic apple, pear and peach cider, from Guysborough."

"I didn't know your winery made non-alcoholic drinks. This is really exceptional. So fruity and fizzy. Where do you get the peaches from?"

"We have an orchard in America."

"Hence the name?" Tamsin asked, referring to the label on the bottle.

"Yes, *'Orchard Grove'* is the brand name we use for this as well as for a few other beverages we produce."

"I had no idea."

Tamsin loved the look of the Guysborough bottles. Their English sparkling wine came in dark green bottles and this cider was bottled in brown glass.

Both the bottles and the colours reminded her of the smooth sea glass she would occasionally find as a child on beaches in Kent.

"Well, it's exceptional, Ben," she said. "You should all be so proud."

"I can't wait to share these drinks with our customers, once the restaurant launches."

The restaurant was due to open in four months and still didn't have a name, or a location, but she didn't want to ruin the mood by mentioning any of that.

They walked over to the balcony and took in the view of the main harbour of Monte Carlo. It was breathtaking. So many boats bobbed gently on the water. To be on time for Basil's party, they would need to leave soon.

"I've called down for Kiki and Tara to come up and do

your hair and make-up. Have you decided what you are wearing tonight?" Ben asked.

"I have indeed." From the minute she tried it on in the boutique, Tamsin knew that the turquoise gown was the right one for a special, personal event, and that was tonight. The silk taffeta of the crinoline shone in luminescent pink and blue, like an opal, and it would look glorious with her new engagement ring. "It's going to be the turquoise dress."

"Excellent choice. I knew from the start that was the one you favoured," Ben said.

"It is. And, Ben..." Tamsin said as she looked down at the engagement ring from Graff on her hand. "This is the most exquisite ring. Thank you." She leaned over to kiss him. Holding her hand out in front of her, she admired the ten carat Asscher cut diamond with the emerald cut baguettes of blue sapphires, a unique take on the traditional engagement ring. It was stunning.

"For you, anything. Shall we?" and he motioned towards the door of the suite, so they could get ready for the party.

As soon as they entered the room, there was a knock on the hotel door.

"It must be Kiki," Ben said.

Both Kiki and Tara arrived together and within thirty minutes, having styled both of their hair and Tamsin's make-up, Tamsin and Ben looked their best. Ben was dressed in white tie, and Tamsin was glowing, she was so excited.

"I have an idea," Ben said. "Why don't I call the hotel photographer to come and take some photos of us? I know it's impromptu, but you look gorgeous tonight, Tamsin, and if they come out well enough, we could use them as engagement photos."

"What a great idea!"

When he arrived, the photographer Mauricio asked them to stand and sit in a few locations in the enormous three bed suite with sea views from every room, and he finished with some shots on the balcony, with the harbour lit up beautifully in the background. He shared a view of two of the best photos with them, and they were thrilled.

"They look great, Mauricio. Thank you," said Ben as he walked him to the door and handed him a tip for coming on such short notice. Tamsin noticed, and thought what a gentleman Ben was. He always considered other people and their feelings. She adored him.

They went downstairs to the lobby, and were greeted by a driver, to take them to the yacht. It wasn't far, but too far to walk in the stiletto heels Tamsin was wearing. And, being a slightly breezy evening, the wind would blow Tamsin's hair around, so Ben had considered that as well when booking a car.

"Are we going to tell people that we're engaged, or leave it for now?" he asked.

"Let's tell Basil, but then keep it to ourselves, until we tell our parents."

They boarded the yacht and found Basil on the deck, having a cigarette and holding a whiskey.

"Ben, get over here!" he said as he called him over with his arm held out.

"Uh-oh, he's already had a few drinks, I'm afraid," Ben

said quietly. "Normally Basil is the most reserved of my friends – until he has a drink that is. But he's harmless. Just gets a bit loud. Stephen will usually help steady him out, if he needs to sleep it off."

They walked over to Basil through a crowd of people. It didn't look like there would be a formal dinner tonight, as Tamsin had been expecting. Luckily they had eaten earlier in their suite.

"Tamsin, this is Basil Crozier, Lord Redhill. Basil, let me introduce you to Tamsin Davies, my fiancée."

"What?!" Basil said and leaned in to kiss Tamsin on the cheek. "You sly devil, Ben! We've all been waiting to meet you for weeks, Tamsin. And now, you two are engaged?"

"Yes. It's nice to meet you, Basil. What a lovely yacht you have," Tamsin said, as she looked around, taking in the three decks of the super yacht.

"Thank you, Tamsin. There's been a change of plans. No formal dinner tonight. I could not make the time to sort that out. But canapes are everywhere. I'm even serving your sparkling wine tonight, Ben."

"Listen, don't mention the engagement to anyone, Basil. Ok? You can tell Stephen, but no one else. Where is he, by the way?"

Stephen, Basil's partner, was talking to other guests across the deck.

"Your secret is safe with me, Ben. No telling the papers, or anyone who will tell them. Right?" he asked as he leaned on Ben. It was obvious that Basil had already had too much to drink and it was only eight-thirty, so he'd not be awake to ring in the new year.

Stephen came over to say hello.

"Ben, how are you? Happy New Year! This must be Tamsin. Am I right?"

"Spot on, Stephen," he said as they shook hands. "I'll tell you, since Basil is likely to either forget or tell everyone. Tamsin and I are engaged."

"What excellent news! Congratulations to you both," he said and leaned in to kiss Tamsin on the cheek. "Nice dress, Tamsin. Dior?"

"Thank you. Yes."

"You look stunning. Must go say hello to others, but please mingle and enjoy yourselves. Sorry we cancelled dinner, but Basil just clean forgot to do anything to organize it and by the time I asked if he had, it was too late."

"Not a problem. We've had dinner and will find something to munch on."

"Basil seems nice," said Tamsin, after Stephen left. "Quite gregarious."

"Yes, he's a great friend. Since the photos of us appeared in the tabloids, he has been asking to meet you. So I'm glad your hotel got flooded and you had to come here to Monte Carlo with me."

"I'm not sure I *had* to come, since I could be enjoying a massive party with the DJ client of mine in Shoreditch tonight."

"That's right! I forgot about that. Didn't he invite you to another event as well?"

"Yes, in February. In Liverpool."

"Will still be cold and likely wet at that time in Liverpool. Where is it being held?"

"Some massive warehouse he uses there. But I'd like to go to his beach rave in January in Ibiza. It's invite only and he hasn't asked me to that."

"That sounds like fun. I'll go with you if you can snag an invite."

"Ok, I'll try."

They said hello to several people Ben knew, and while Ben introduced her as his girlfriend, a few people's eyes strayed to her left ring finger, but no one asked if they were engaged.

As the countdown to midnight started, they gathered together on the main deck with the other guests and all ensured they each had a glass to raise.

"Eight, seven..." they all said as a chorus.

"Three, two, one!"

"Happy New Year!" they all shouted, and Ben and Tamsin kissed.

"Let's go," Ben whispered in Tamsin's ear and they left the yacht and headed back to the hotel in the chauffeured car.

❄ ❄ ❄

"That was fun," said Tamsin as she undressed.

"Yes, I enjoyed it as well."

"What a gorgeous yacht Basil has. How do you know him?"

"Eton. Let's talk tomorrow about our wedding plans," said Ben as he faced Tamsin and stroked her hair, then hopped onto the bed and beckoned her to join him.

CHAPTER 73

New Year's Day

When they woke up, the sun was shining through all the windows of the suite and the water was sparkling like diamonds. It was a magical sight to see. Tamsin yawned and stretched, and noticed Ben was gone from the bed. He was always up earlier than she was.

She took a shower and when she came out, Ben was back, and breakfast had been delivered. On her plate was a jewellery box, and she wondered what it could be.

"Morning, darling," Ben said as he came into the dining room.

"Morning, sexy," she replied. "What's this?" she asked, pointing to the green box.

"Something to go with your ring."

"Should I open it now?"

"Yes, go ahead."

Tamsin had no idea what could be inside, but thought it might be a necklace. Opening the box, she was stunned by what she saw. It was a diamond necklace with a large blue sapphire and three rows of diamonds, all in different cuts. It was breathtaking.

"Honestly, Ben, you spoil me."

"I know, but it's my pleasure. Let me help you," and he got up to help her put the necklace on.

She held his hand once he closed the clasp and he bent down to kiss her.

"This is really something."

"I wanted you to have a necklace of your own, not just borrow from the estate jewels. This can become a new family heirloom. I also had it engraved," and he pointed to the clasp, where it read 'TD&HSJ,' their initials. "Now, what are you going to do about uni, Mrs. Smythe-Jones-to-be?"

"Let's see. I need to contact the University of Texas and tell them I'm not coming, for a start. Where are we going to live, Ben?"

"Where would you like to live? Kensington, or Oxford?"

"Can you really live in Kensington, since you have to get the restaurant off the ground? And speaking of that, are your solicitors any closer to getting what they need to complete the purchase?"

"I can keep a base in Kensington, but living in Oxford is probably better. Although I could continue going back and forth for a month or so, until the building purchase has completed. And I don't know the status of the legal checks, so I'll have to call them this week, if they are open."

"I still have City University in London as an option, if I hurry up and decide soon. It's the only option once I turn down the scholarship to the States. But for that to work, I'd need to be in London."

"Do you want to go to City? What about studying at Oxford? You could apply there for the spring intake."

"I'll never get into Oxford, Ben. I don't have the grades."

"What about Oxford Brookes then? Do they have law?"

"Law conversion is what I need. And yes, I would imagine they do."

"How about going there? Then you can move in with me at Lavender Cottage, and we can stay in London for another month or two while the restaurant gets fitted out."

"I could try that. I'm sure I'd be accepted there. But first, I need to tell my parents about our engagement and I expect you need to tell your father and Pepper."

"Yes, well, Papa is away with Pepper in Aspen, skiing. They will be gone for a while. I think you could tell your parents, and I'll call Father. Then maybe your parents could come to Tansley Hall when my father and Pepper return, so I can meet them and we can all get acquainted, including Granny."

"That sounds like a plan. I'll go home to Margate if that's ok, and then I'll take the train back to London..."

"I can send a car for you so you can bring more of your things to Kensington."

"Perfect."

"Now, let's go on the balcony and enjoy this glorious January sunshine!"